"I am a prince of this realm."
"What is a prince?" she inquired breathlessly.

I hear later that he killed two giants, a raging bull, and a wild boar, and thus earned for himself the hand of the king's daughter and half a kingdom, but I wonder if that can possibly be true.

"Pay him!" I shouted. "Pay him what you promised, or by heaven I'll let him pipe your children away!"

Prince Hyacinth, as they inappropriately named the child, grew to manhood being assured constantly that his was a most magnificent nose—one to be imitated but never matched. I was endlessly entertained by the stories the courtiers invented to justify their admiration of the enormous beak which preceded the prince wherever he went.

He is mad still, though usually quite gentle and biddable. But I never trust him with an axe.

Her actual name is Elinor, you know. Somehow the ridiculous name of Cinderella has become attached to her, as the "wicked" appellation has to me, and neither is true.

We were rather pleased when my cousin stole the beans. We were sure he'd sell them to some poor soul, who'd soon come climbing up the beanstalk and provide us with a meal. We looked forward to that.

Happily Ever After, And All That

Varied Tales

Jackie Shank

Illustrated by Linda Alexander

Strawberry Hill Press

Copyright © 1997 by Jackie Shank
Illustrations Copyright © 1997 by Linda Alexander

Strawberry Hill Press
3848 S.E. Division Street
Portland, Oregon 97202-1641

Cover design by Ku, Fu-sheng
Typeset and designed by Wordwrights, Portland, Oregon

Manufactured in the United States of America

Library of Congress Cataloging-in-Publication Data

Shank, Jackie, 1926-
    Happily ever after, and all that : varied tales / Jackie Shank : illustrations by Linda Alexander.
        p.   cm.
    ISBN 0-89407-108-4 (trade paper)
    1. Fairy tales—Adaptations. I. Alexander, Linda. II. Title.
PS3569.H33257H37   1997
813'.54—dc20   96-30550
                                     CIP

For Stan

And thanks to the Monday Writing Group

Table of Contents

Introduction 9
Rapunzel 11
The Frog Prince 17
Snow White and the Seven Dwarfs 23
Two in a Sack 27
The Three Wishes 31
Trusty John 35
The Twelve Dancing Princesses 39
The Brave Little Tailor 45
The Three Bears 49
How the Sea Became Salt 53
Snow White and Rose Red 57
The Pied Piper 61
Beauty and the Beast 65
The Three Little Pigs 71
Prince Hyacinth and the Dear Little Princess 75
Hansel and Gretel 81
The Three Billy Goats Gruff 85
The Goose Girl 89
The Princess on the Glass Hill 93
The Girl Who Set Out to Learn About Fear 97
The Fish and the Ring 103
Cinderella 107
The Boy Who Found Fear at Last 113
Jack and the Beanstalk 119
Rumpelstiltzkin 123

Introduction

It occurred to me, after teaching elementary school for some years, that if the best way to learn to read is by reading, perhaps the best way to learn to write would be by writing. So I developed the idea of a "Rough Book," a spiral notebook in which teacher and student alike would write for ten minutes every day, directly after lunch.

These books were never graded, though occasionally we shared our writing with the class. The Rough Book was for practice in getting words on paper, without having to worry about spelling, grammar, handwriting, or writing something teacher wouldn't like. Content wasn't as important as letting the words and thoughts flow.

I usually put a suggested topic on the chalkboard, for the inevitable youngster who didn't know what to write about. One day, about eight years ago, I ran completely out of ideas, and asked for suggestions from the class. One of the girls said, "We could write fairy tales," which struck me as an interesting possibility.

"Rewrite a fairy tale," I wrote on the chalkboard. The little girl and I did just that. I don't know what happened to her story, but mine was the nucleus for this book of re-told folk tales.

Her face took
on the alert,
intelligent
expression
of a
browsing
sheep.

Rapunzel

While walking my horse in a desultory way through the forest one morning, I heard a quavery old voice call out, "Rapunzel, Rapunzel, let down your golden hair."

This sounded so intriguing that I decided to investigate. In a short time I found a branching trail from the one I was riding on, and soon came upon the most curious sight I have seen in all my twenty years.

In the midst of a clearing was a tower. Climbing up a ladder on the outside of the tower, toward the single visible window at the top, was a gray-haired crone. Leaning from the window was a most incredibly beautiful young woman, flaxen haired, pink cheeked, blue eyed, looking like a damsel from some ancient tale.

I watched the old lady reach the window, and crawl in, with some assistance from the shining beauty. Then I dismounted, saw to the welfare of my horse, and sat down under a nearby tree to see what would happen next.

After a time, when the sun was well past noon, the old woman climbed back down the ladder, and went down the trail I had found earlier, and which I had prudently vacated. The radiant being in the window above drew up the ladder and began to sing, a simple but quite lovely melody.

I searched in vain for an entry to the tower, discovering that there was no opening other than the window at the top. Wishing to converse with the dazzling occupant, and recalling the words of the aged woman, I determined to see what happened if I repeated them.

"Rapunzel, Rapunzel," I called, "Let down your golden hair."

Immediately the end of the ladder was thrown down from above. I noticed that the rope was made of a material of about the same color as the maiden's hair, though closer examination showed that it was simply a yellowish fiber. I climbed up, sincerely hoping, since I was clearly heavier than the old lady, that the upper end was firmly anchored. It was.

When I reached the top, only slightly out of breath, I heard a little voice exclaim, "Oh! You are not my foster mother!"

"No indeed," I replied, sweeping a gallant bow to the stunning creature before me, who had assumed a position of mild alarm. "In fact," I added, "I am a prince of this realm."

Her face took on the alert, intelligent expression of a browsing sheep. "What is a prince?" she inquired breathlessly.

"I am the second son of the king of this realm," I answered.

"King?" she asked. "Realm?"

"The king is the ruler of the country." Her expression remained blankly puzzled, but willing to learn. "He is in charge of everything that happens," I continued, exaggerating slightly.

"Oh. Like my foster mother."

"No. Well, yes, but on a rather larger scale. Your foster mother controls you, and this tower, and perhaps the clearing around it. My father governs the entire country."

"Country?"

"The realm."

"But what is a realm?" she asked perplexedly. "You mentioned that word before."

Aha, I thought, a feat of memory. There is a rudimentary intelligence here. Taking her hand, I led her to the window.

"All the land you see, as far as you can see, and farther, in all directions, is my father's realm." I held up my hand before she could ask the next question. "And a realm is the same as a country." Puzzled frown. "Two words that mean the same thing," I explained, as patiently as I could.

The next plaintive question turned out not to be the one I was expecting. "You said all the land in all directions, but I can only see in one direction from this tower."

"If there were more windows, so that you could see in all directions," I sighed, "then all the land you could see would be but a small part of my father's realm."

"Rapunzel!" came an angry voice from just below the window. "Why have you let down your golden hair when I didn't...Aha!" the crone cried, spying me, "I have caught you red-handed!"

"Red-handed?" came the inevitable piteous question, as I helped the old lady into the tower room.

"What are you doing here, you miserable wretch?" she shouted at me.

I drew myself up. "I was, ah, conversing with your, um, ward, Madame."

She smiled a particularly evil smile. "Oh yes," she snarled, "and thinking of carrying her off with you to boot, I'll wager."

I was horrified, appalled. "Good grief no, Madame," I replied, "certainly not!"

"Is she not beautiful enough for you then?" she asked.

"Perfectly lovely," I said, "utterly enchanting," muttering under my breath, "to look at."

"You wouldn't reconsider?" she asked wistfully.

"Under no circumstances. I am betrothed to Princess Cordelia, Madame, and we are to be married at mid-winter. I am not my father's heir," I added, "but she is her father's only child, and when she is queen of her realm, I shall be her consort."

"Realm!" came the little voice from the beautiful empty face, "I remember that word. But what does 'betrothed' mean, and what is a 'Cordelia'? And is a princess the same as a prince?"

I began to back gracefully toward the window. "Ladies," I bowed, "I bid you farewell."

"I will put an enchantment upon you," the ancient witch began, "which will compel you to forget your Cordelia and to fall head over heels in love with my Rapunzel..."

"Oh Madame, I beg you!" I fell upon my knees in entreaty. "Do not be so cruel! Consider my father's feelings. Consider Cordelia's father's feelings. Consider, if you will, that Cordelia is a far more appropriate name for a princess than Rapunzel. Wherever did you get such an outlandish name?"

"Do not seek to divert me with nonsense," she said. "I must get this creature off my hands before I lose my mind, and you present a precious opportunity, one which may not come again."

I was about to plead once more for mercy, but then bethought me of my cousin Alistair. "Ah!" I said, "I have the solution."

"You do?"

"I do." I beckoned her away from the bewildered Rapunzel. "I have a relative, Madame, who is as empty-headed, and very nearly as beautiful, as your ward. He is the despair of the court, for no young woman of any station can bear to spend more than fifteen minutes in his company. His mother has very nearly given up any notions of seeing him married and thus off her hands."

"But I don't see..." she began.

"Consider," I said, "my father, and Alistair's mother, in their profound gratitude, will reward you handsomely for Rapunzel. They will pay for keepers, er, retainers, to care for the happy couple. You will be free to fill this tower with toads if you will—or butterflies and flowers," I added hastily, seeing her begin to frown.

She smiled and extended her hand. "Rapunzel," she said, turning to that mystified beauty, "you are about to be happily married, you fortunate young creature."

"Married?"

And so it happened that two weddings took place at mid-winter. Cordelia and I were married in her father's palace. And Rapunzel and Alistair, who had taken to each other immediately, in his mother's castle. I trust that they are as happy as we.

It is I, Your
Highness. The frog.
Down here...

The Frog Prince

Once upon a time I was a prince with a curse on me. The curse was Mother's fault, though she didn't mean to do it. It happened because one day when she was feeling out of sorts, she insulted my father's sister, the witch. It doesn't pay to insult a witch, of course. Mother apologized, and Aunt Maud seemed to accept her apology, so Mother never gave it another thought. But Aunt Maud did; oh yes, memory like an elephant, that woman.

In the finest witchy tradition, she took her vengeance at my christening. She was seen to make some mysterious signs with her hands, and heard to mumble some mysterious words, but she was an eccentric old thing, and no one paid much attention. We found out all about it at my twenty-first birthday party.

What a hilarious day that was for Aunt Maud! That was the day I turned into a frog. Mother was hysterical, and my little brother laughed so hard he got the hiccups. You can imagine how I felt. The only person who stayed calm was my father, and he at least had the presence of mind to ask the dear old thing if there was any way to lift the curse.

"Of course, dear, we always leave people a way out. Makes it more interesting—to see if they can do it. All that's required is that he persuade a princess to kiss him. She needn't even be a beautiful princess, just so she's of royal blood. Oh, by the way, he'll be able to talk to princesses, but no one else will be able to understand a croak, er, word he says." She laughed her way out of the royal party room, and we never saw her again. I've always rather hoped something awful happened to her.

There seemed little use in hanging about the palace, especially since no one could understand anything I said, so I went to live in a pool at the bottom of the royal garden in a neighboring country. That, I thought, is where one is most likely to encounter a princess. Ha, ha. Girls came to the pool, lots of them, but never a one who could understand me. Not for I don't know how many years—one loses track of time when one is a frog in a pool at the bottom of a royal garden.

But one joyous day I heard the sound of ladies' voices, and one called the other "Your Highness." I held my breath, hoping they would come close enough that I could talk to the princess. As she approached, I could see that she was swinging a locket on a chain. Suddenly the chain broke, and the locket flew into my pool. Hurrah, I thought, as I dove in to retrieve it, that will bring them closer.

The princess sent her lady in waiting to find it, but you can bet I didn't give it to her. In fact, I kept it hidden, hoping to lure the princess closer. And I succeeded. As she approached I spoke up.

"Your Highness," I said, "I will return your locket to you in return for one small favor."

"Eek!" was her response, which I thought did not bode well for any future relationship. "Who is that? Who's talking?"

"It is I, Your Highness. The frog. Down here, Your Highness. Please, Your Highness, just listen to my story!" I exclaimed, as the poor girl began to look distraught. "I am a prince, under a curse to remain in frog form until a princess kisses me. I will return your locket, which fell into the pool, if you will do this one small thing for me. Please, just one kiss, Your Highness."

"Yuck!" she remarked. "I don't know that I want the locket that badly. You keep it."

"Your Highness," the lady in waiting inquired plaintively, "are you talking to me? I don't have your locket, and I certainly couldn't keep it if I did. It was a gift from your father, and he'd never tolerate your giving it to me."

"No, silly, I'm talking to the frog. Didn't your hear what he said?"

"Er, no, Your Highness. Uh, what did he say?" The lady in waiting put her wrist to the princess's forehead in a diagnostic way, but the princess brushed her off.

"I'm not sick! And I think maybe I'll do it. I've kissed some really ugly boys, and the frog is actually kind of cute."

By this time the poor lady in waiting was looking a bit glassy-eyed, but the princess disregarded her.

"But I don't want to do it here, where no one will see but you. Think what a sensation, to change a frog into a handsome prince in front of the whole court."

The princess frowned and turned to me. "You were a handsome prince, weren't you? Are you sure this will work? I don't want to make a fool of myself."

"As to the first, Your Highness, I was accounted tolerably presentable, and as to the second, I have only the word of my Aunt Maud. She was a wicked old witch, but a witch of her word. So I think it will work. I beg you to try it. I'm so tired of being a frog. There's simply nothing to do down here by the pool."

"Very well," she said, "give me the locket and we'll go. It's almost dinner time anyway."

"Just a moment, if you please. I have hidden the locket, but when you have turned me back into a prince, I will be happy to show you where it is. Meanwhile, let us by all means go to dinner."

So we did. I rode in the princess's pocket, and as the royal family and their guests were being seated, she put me on the table and said she had an announcement to make. She then related my story, and leaned down and kissed me.

"Eek!" she shrieked. (This girl had a limited vocabulary, didn't she?)

"What's wrong now?" I asked. I could tell I had been changed back into a prince—and don't think I didn't feel silly, standing there on the table. My gosh, I thought as I got down, maybe I don't have any clothes on, but a quick check reassured me.

"Oh," she wailed, "you're old! Old, old, old! I thought you'd be young and I could marry you and go to live with you in your kingdom, and get away from this stuffy boring court, but you're old!"

"Now then young lady," her father remonstrated, "you are being unfair. He's very little older than I."

"That's what I mean!"

While they discussed my age, I sneaked a look in one of the mirrors with which the hall was hung. She was right, I must have been a frog longer than I thought. I was, in appearance at least, about her father's age.

"Your Highness," I said to the princess, "I don't recall having asked you to marry me. Just to kiss me, to break the curse."

While she pouted, I turned to her father. "What I'd like to do, sir, is borrow a horse and go see what's been happening in my own kingdom while I've been gone."

So the king loaned me a horse, a sword, some money, and a cloak, and after returning the princess's locket, I made my way to my home.

There I found that my father had died, and my younger brother was king. It could be said that he had usurped my throne, but when the heir is turned into a frog and disappears he must be presumed dead, and a kingdom needs a ruler.

After he had made it quite clear that he would tolerate no interference with his rule, and I had made it quite clear that I had no desire to reclaim my throne, we got along satisfactorily. In fact, he had a handsome young son about the age of the princess, so I suggested that perhaps he would like to look into the marriage possibilities.

The upshot of that was that my nephew and my princess were married the following spring.

At the wedding, I was able to get better acquainted with the princess's lady in waiting. It turned out that Mathilda was as bored with waiting on her royal highness as I was with avoiding my touchy brother. So after we were married we took up beekeeping in a different kingdom altogether, and have lived thus happily for many years.

Snow White and the Seven Dwarfs

By the time the Prince and Snow White arrive at the palace, I will be in the next kingdom, having been warned by my faithful mirror. I wish them joy of this miserable little country. May they spawn many brats, and may the brats fight over the succession to the throne, and may the kingdom be broken into as many parts as there are brats.

Actually, I have no personal quarrel with Snow White. She was but a child when I married her weakling father, who soon passed away in a fever of confusion. Strangely, the few courtiers who opposed my appointment to the Regency died of the same sort of wasting fever, and thereafter there was no difficulty about who was to rule.

Snow White was a sweet and biddable girl, kindly to all, charming to everyone high or low. As long as she was but a popular child, I had no quarrel with her, and let her be. But the day my mirror told me she was fairer than I, I knew I would have to be rid of her. Few will flock to the banner of a mere child, however lovable. But many may be persuaded to support a beautiful young woman, and that I would not tolerate.

"Hunter," I said to one of the few about the court whom I trusted implicitly, "why do you not take the princess to the forest on such a lovely day? I will have cook pack a luncheon for the two of you. Enjoy yourself. And if you should tragically return alone, a bag of gold will find its way to your quarters."

That evening he returned, dejected and forlorn, riding his horse and leading Snow White's. They had dismounted in a sunny glade by a stream, he explained, and had eaten their picnic lunch. He lay down on the grass in the sun for a short nap, while Snow White gathered flowers. When he awakened, she was gone. He searched and called, but could find no trace of the girl, except a kerchief floating in the stream. At dark he had given up and ridden back to the palace.

That night when I checked with my mirror, I found that the princess had somehow crossed the stream and wandered off to the west. Next day, therefore, Hunter led a large but unsuccessful search party to the east of the picnic glade. The kingdom went into mourning, Hunter took his gold and moved to the kingdom to the north, and I, with relief, went back to ruling.

Some weeks later, on looking into my mirror, I found to my horrified surprise that the girl was alive and well, and living with a group of seven dwarfs deep in the forest. Not only that, but as I watched her I realized that she was quite content, and that the dwarfs were simply delighted with her. This would never do. Sooner or later, someone would come along who recognized her, causing me all manner of trouble.

I therefore disguised myself as an old crone, injected poison into a shiny red apple, and took my way to the dwelling of the dwarfs, making sure that I arrived while they were about whatever business they had that took them out of the cottage.

Leaving my horse concealed in the forest, I approached the hut afoot, panting and hobbling in well-simulated exhaustion.

The simpering child was of course most sympathetic, bidding me rest my weary old bones while she fetched me a drink of cold water. And would I like some broth? A piece of bread and some cheese, perhaps?

"No, pretty child," I quavered, "the fresh water and an opportunity to rest are all I require. Thank you so much for your kindness. As a reward, I beg you to choose an apple for yourself. No, no, I have plenty. Do take this one, isn't it pretty?"

After some hesitation, she accepted the apple, and upon my urging bit into it. And then an appalling thing happened. She swallowed but one bite and collapsed instantly into the deep sleep induced by so small an amount. Weakling! Too puny to stay awake long enough to take the second, fatal bite. And I with nothing but my hands to insure her death. But as I reached for her throat, I heard the singing of the dwarfs as they returned. Hastily, I retreated from the cottage, mounted my horse, and rode furiously back to the palace.

Perhaps, I thought, they would believe her dead, and bury her. Unpleasant for her, of course, when she awoke, but safer for me. A glance in the mirror, however, disabused me of that hope. No, the silly creatures, somehow detecting that she but slept, created a bier for her with a crystal cover, and placed it reverently in the clearing in front of their hut. They constructed a roofed shed over it, I presume to shelter it from the elements, and there she lay.

I knew that I had but months to arrange a secure future for myself, for Snow White would awaken one day, and if she was loving and forgiving, the dwarfs would not be. They had known, I discovered in listening to their discussions, who their charming visitor was, and strongly suspected the identity of her poisoner. Why, I wonder, did I not collect the remains of the poisoned apple before I fled? Ah me, it's the little mistakes that trip us up, is it not?

When my preparations were made, I watched my mirror carefully, unwilling to flee my position of power and comfort before it was necessary.

By a remarkable coincidence, the day she began to awaken was the very day the prince from the neighboring kingdom happened past the dwarfs' hut while on a hunt with a group of companions. And who, I wonder, gave him permission to hunt on our lands? Never mind, it matters not.

For of course he spied Snow White lying on her bier, and of course he lifted the crystal cover, and equally of course he kissed her. A romantic soul such as he could never resist such a gesture. And of course, that was the moment she chose to awaken. They will go to their graves believing that his kiss defeated the effects of the poison, poor innocents.

I watched the dwarfs return to their home, the rejoicing among them at Snow White's recovery, and without having to listen to their discussions, I took note of the moment when their joy turned to thoughts of vengeance. That was the moment for which I had been waiting.

Clutching my mirror, I hurried to the stables, where I commanded the boy to saddle my horse, and load my already prepared personal possessions on a strong pack horse. Clothes, food, and many jewels I took with me, and some gold, but gold is too heavy to carry more than a bit while fleeing one's enemies.

By the time the princess, her prince, and company reach the palace, I shall be safe in the kingdom to the south. There lives, just beyond that kingdom, an aging monarch who is in great need of a beautiful and able queen to succor him in his last days.

On this particular day, I took the net and caught an unusually large and handsome crane.

Two in a Sack

You wouldn't believe what I've put up with nearly all our married life. I can't tell you when it started, for she surely wasn't a shrew when we were wed, but for the past several years she's nagged and scolded and even hit me with her broom, until I don't know how I stood it. Well, in fact, I didn't. I'd leave the house, with her voice going on and on about what a ne'er-do-well I was, and a poor provider and all.

Usually when I left I'd take a fishing line, or a bird net, to try to catch something to placate her. On this particular day, I took the net, and caught an unusually large and handsome crane.

"Let me go," he said, "and I'll prove my gratitude."

I was moderately surprised to hear him talk, but we live in strange times, so I replied that I would instead take him home to my wife, who then might cease her scolding for a time.

"Oh ho," he exclaimed, "if that's your problem, come home with me and I'll give you something better to quiet her."

"I don't want her harmed," I began, but he interrupted me.

"For heaven's sake, man, untangle me from this net and come along. I have no intention of harming anyone, and what I will give you will be to your advantage."

Well, he was very persuasive, and rather large, so I agreed. His home was some distance away, and by the time we reached it I was tired and hungry and thirsty. He took a plain-looking sack from a hook, and said, "Two out of the sack!" and out crept two pretty boys, who proceeded to pull from the sack a table, a chair, linens, and such food and drink as I had never seen. We certainly do live in strange times, I thought, but when the crane urged me to fall to, I can tell you I needed little encouragement.

When I had finished eating he said, "Two into the sack!" and the two boys crept back into the sack, taking the table and its fittings with them.

"Now take this sack to your wife," said the crane. "It is my thanks to you for freeing me from your net."

I was delighted to do as he asked, and set out at once. Since it was late, however, I decided to spend the night with a cousin who lived a short distance away.

She was not pleased to see me, but she rather grudgingly offered me a meal. I rejected her offer in favor of showing off the powers of my fine sack. My wife's favorite word for me for is fool, and perhaps she is right, for it never occurred to me that my cousin would substitute a different sack for the marvelous one given me by the crane.

When I awoke the next morning I took what I thought was my sack, and happily went home. Before my old woman could begin to scold I put the sack on the floor and said, "Two out of the sack!"

Well, of course, nothing at all happened, and of course she screamed at me for a fool, which I did not enjoy—even though for once I agreed with her. And also of course, I knew what had happened, but I couldn't think how to get the real food sack from my cousin. So in order to get away from my wife's scolding, and because I didn't know what else to do, I went to visit the crane. He laughed at me, but he also gave me another sack, with the admonition to take better care of it.

I became hungry on my way home, and also felt that a test of the sack would not be out of order, so I said, "Two out of the sack!" And out came not two pretty boys with wonderful things to eat and drink, but two burly rascals who proceeded to beat me with sticks. Strange times indeed! You may believe that I was in a great rush to say, "Two into the sack!" You may also believe that I now knew how to retrieve the original sack from my cousin.

When I arrived at her house she wondered sweetly what wonderful sack I had this time, and so of course I demonstrated. When she had been persuaded to return my food sack to me, I called off the ruffians with their sticks. We then sat down happily to a delicious meal, but believe me, I slept that night with both sacks in the bed with me.

When I got home the next day my wife began to scold in her usual way, but I silenced her by producing the food sack and providing her with a lovely dinner. After dinner, since she had mellowed a bit, I told her all my adventures. She was amused by the tale, as you may suppose.

Since she had always scolded because she was hungry, we now get along remarkably well.

Nor do we worry about thieves stealing our food sack.

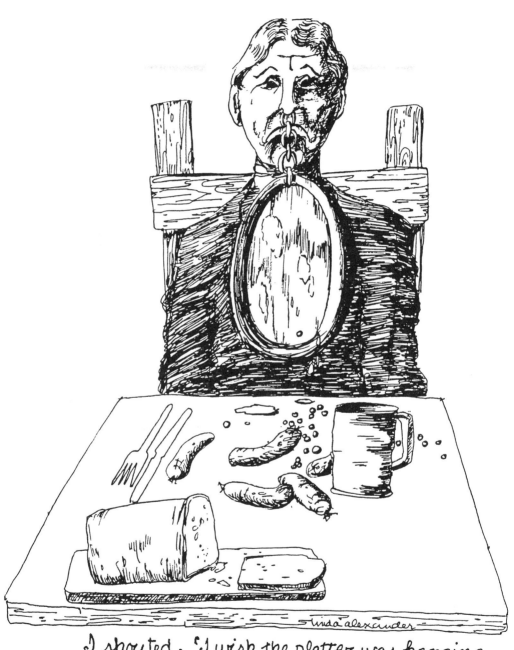

I shouted, 'I wish the platter was hanging on your nose, you old Fool!'

The
Three Wishes

*W*hat a silly thing to do! We had three wishes, my husband and I, and we could have had anything, anything in the world. A splendid wish might have been for money, a great deal of it. We could have wished for more wishes. Or for a lovely home, servants, carriages, rich clothing, all the food we could eat, or...ah me, what is the use of complaining. It is all over now, all our golden chances. And it is all Bert's fault. Well, mostly his fault.

We received the three wishes in the first place because my fisherman husband caught a magic fish. I know, that sounds incredible, but it is true, it really is. When he hauled in the net one day there was an especially big, gold-colored fish, who said, "If you let me go I will give you three wishes."

Well, even slow-pated Bert could understand that if a fish could talk it could probably grant three wishes, so he let it go. Personally, I would have kept it and made it give me more wishes, but I am more intelligent than Bert. I married beneath myself.

He came rushing home to tell me all about it, and we agreed that we had better think and plan seriously and carefully before we made our wishes, to be sure we got the most out of them. We talked far into the night, deciding what would be best.

When we got up in the morning I made our usual breakfast of porridge. I supposed we would make our wishes after breakfast, as we had planned.

But what did that clod do? He sighed and said, "Porridge again! How I wish I had a platter of sausages."

And behold, there it was on the table, a precious wish for a platter of sausages!

It made me so angry that I shouted, without thinking, "I wish the platter was hanging on your nose, you old fool!" And there, of course, was the platter hanging from a chain which was firmly embedded in Bert's nose!

I was so furious by then, at both of us, that I would gladly have left the thing hanging there—or pulled it off bodily—but of course he wished it off, and that was our third wish.

We could have had...Well, we don't, so it is back to fishing for Bert, and porridge for breakfast. Maybe he will catch that golden fish again, and then we will get three more wishes. And maybe we will use them more wisely next time.

And maybe tomorrow the sun will rise in the west and set in the east.

To my astonishment, the room was empty, save for a portrait of the most exquisitely beautiful girl I had ever seen.

Trusty John

*J*ust before my father, the king, died, he called for me.

"Hilarion, my son," he said. "You must trust my servant, John, in all things. He will protect and guide you well."

After Father had been buried with all due pomp, John gave me a tour of the palace, showing me everything from the meanest attic to the dungeons far below. I noticed, however, that he passed one locked room without showing me its contents. When we went by that door for the third time, I demanded to know the reason.

"Oh," he said, "there is nothing of importance in there."

"Well," I said, "let's have a look at this nothing."

He hesitated, saying, "Your father, sire..."

I drew myself up. "Despite my father's apparent wishes, I will see what is in that room."

"Very well," he said, and unlocked the door, with obvious misgivings. I went in, hardly knowing what kind of horror to expect. To my astonishment, the room was empty, save for a portrait of the most exquisitely beautiful girl I had ever seen.

"Who is this divine creature?" I demanded.

"That is the Princess of the Golden Roof, sire," he answered reluctantly.

"I believe I have fallen in love with her," I said. "I must meet her."

"Oh sire," he said, wringing his hands, "she lives across the sea, and..."

"And?"

"And she loves only gold, sire. She has said she will marry the man who brings her the rarest and most elegant gold articles. So far, no one has satisfied her. Your father..."

"Would not have approved, I'm sure," I completed his sentence. "Else why try to keep me from seeing her portrait? Nevertheless, we will

do what we can to win her hand. We have a great deal of gold on hand,
I saw it. Do we not have skilled goldsmiths, as well?" He nodded. "Then
see to it that they create the finest objects in the world. Then we shall
see."

John was a trustworthy servant, and did as I commanded, so that I
was overwhelmed when I saw what he had accomplished. Vases, bowls,
birds, fish, goblets, crowns, necklaces, rings—all magnificently wrought.

"If this doesn't bring her round, nothing will, and I shall die of
unrequited love," I said, only half-joking.

We loaded the gold on a splendid ship and sailed for the land of the
Golden Roof. The Princess Gloria, when at last we reached her shore,
was even more ravishingly beautiful than her portrait conveyed, and I
thought perhaps I really would die of love if she refused me. However,
when she was at last persuaded to visit our ship, she was so impressed
with the quantity and quality of the gold pieces we had brought that she
agreed to marry me and accompany me back to my own kingdom. I was
the happiest man in the world.

When we reached the shore of my kingdom, there was a carriage
awaiting Gloria, and a splendid chestnut horse for me. But my trusty
John leaped upon the horse, drew a pistol from a holster, and shot it
dead.

This created consternation among my courtiers, but I told them that
this was my father's trusted servant, and mine, and therefore he must
have had reason for his actions.

When we came to the palace, there was a bridal shirt laid out for me,
but before I could put it on, John took it in gloved hands and threw it
upon the fire. Again my courtiers murmured, and again I excused John
because I trusted him.

After the wedding, a reception and dance was held in the grand
ballroom. All went well until suddenly Gloria turned white and fainted.
Immediately John sprang forward, lifted her, carried her to an adjoining
room, drew some blood from her side and spat it out. Then Gloria sat up
and smiled at me, and I felt sure that this had been a temporary faint due
to excitement.

However, I listened this time to the murmuring of my courtiers,
feeling that John had gone too far, and determined to have him hung. As
he stood upon the gallows, he asked, "May I say a last word, sire?"

I nodded and he continued, "I am unjustly condemned. While we
were at sea, I heard the conversation of three ravens. The first said that
the horse that met you at the dock would kill you, unless he were shot

first, but that anyone who knew this and told it would be turned to stone from the foot to the knee.

"The second said that the bridal shirt would burn you if you put it on, but that anyone who knew this and told it would be turned to stone from the knee to the waist.

"The third said that the bride would die unless someone drew three drops of blood from her right side and spat it out, but that anyone who knew this and told it would be turned to stone from the waist to the top of his head.

"All that I have done, I did for you, sire!" John cried, and turned to stone.

Well then, as you may imagine, I was dreadfully sorry I had not trusted him completely. I had my faithful stone servant carried to the royal suite, and placed in the sitting room, as a reminder to put more faith in a dependable servant.

After Gloria and I had been married for a year, she gave birth to a delightful son, and two years later another son was born. One day when Florian was four and Julian two, playing happily at Trusty John's stone feet, I sighed and said, "Oh John, how sorry I am that I didn't trust you. I miss your sound advice."

"You can bring me back to life if you will, sire," the stone figure said.

I was startled, of course, but delighted, and demanded to know how this might be done.

"If you cut off the heads of your children, and smear me with their blood, I will come back to life," he said.

I was horrified. "Kill my two precious sons!" I cried. "Never! Could I not cut their fingers a little and smear you with that blood?"

"No," the statue said, "for it must be their life blood. Do you not trust me?"

That gave me pause. He had been turned to stone because I had not trusted him, and I was truly sorry. But I found myself unwilling to sacrifice my two boys to return John to life. They were, after all, the heirs to the throne, and the delight of Gloria's life and my own, while John, though honest and reliable, was but a servant. So I refused to do as he said, and he remained stone.

Thereafter I found that I did not care to have him so near to me, and had him carried to the attic. I preferred not to remind my other servants, and my courtiers, that the reward for faithful service to me might be to be turned to stone.

Father would storm in, demanding
to know how we had
contrived to
wear out another
set of
slippers.

The Twelve
Dancing Princesses

*E*very night my sisters and I opened the trap door, descended the stairs, crossed the lake in boats rowed by the enchanted princes, and danced in the beautiful ballroom until our satin slippers were quite worn out. Then we returned to our bedchamber and slept until noon.

When we arose, yawning and stretching, we signaled to the servants to unlock our door and bring us our luncheon. Shortly thereafter, Father would storm in, demanding to know how we had contrived to wear out yet another set of slippers. We always smiled enigmatically and said nothing, for we didn't want to lie to dear Father, but equally we had no desire to tell him the truth.

I am the eldest of the twelve daughters of King Lorenzo and Queen Lucinda. After bearing a dozen of us, trying to produce a son, poor Mother quite gave up, and Father had to resign himself to finding twelve princes, providing twelve dowries, and hoping one of us would marry someone to whom he could, in good conscience, leave the kingdom.

Father said we were impoverishing the country, and unduly enriching the shoemakers of the realm, so he sent forth a proclamation to the effect that whoever could discover how we wore out our shoes could choose one of us to marry. This did not alarm us, for we knew that our secret was perfectly safe. And night after night princes who were ambitious, or curious, or merely overconfident, were locked in our room with us, only to disappear before noon the next day.

Then of course Father had another anxiety in addition to the expense of our shoes. How, he demanded of us, was he to explain their disappearances to the fathers of these princes?

"I shouldn't think you would need to explain, Father," I said. "They must surely come of their own choice, and by this time all the world knows that they somehow vanish overnight. If they are concerned, their fathers need only forbid them to come."

"Leona, I try, but I cannot discourage them," Father replied. "Each thinks he will succeed where the others have failed. Nothing your mother or I says will deter them."

"Well then," I said, "they have only themselves to blame. And no," I added, seeing him draw an angry breath, "I cannot tell you what becomes of them."

To have been perfectly honest, I ought to have said I would not tell, but I assured myself that my statement was mostly true and let it stand.

Next day the gardener's new helper, whose name was Michael, came to our room with quite a nice bouquet. Our youngest sister Lina, who is rather feather-headed, exclaimed at his good looks, at which the rest of us laughed.

"Lina, dear," I explained kindly, "no matter how handsome he may be, a princess may never look at a gardener's helper." Poor Lina was quite quelled, but then she is a timid little thing.

A few nights later, as we were going down the stairs, I in front and the rest behind according to age, Lina cried out that there was someone behind her who had trod on her gown.

"Oh for mercy's sakes, Lina," I said impatiently, "you are always afraid of something. Your dress probably caught on a nail. Who could possibly be behind you?"

Clearly the answer to that was no one, and so we continued on our way. As we crossed the lake, Lina complained that her boat was being rowed more slowly than usual, and the prince who was rowing remarked that the boat seemed awfully low in the water.

"There is probably too much water under the floorboards," I said. "You must be more thorough in your bailing hereafter, Prince."

We danced the night away as always, with the many princes who had tried to discover our secret. They had found out to their sorrow, for now they were enchanted and must remain in the ballroom and dance with us each night. As we came back up the stairs that morning, Lina insisted that someone stepped on her gown again, but we paid no attention.

For a week thereafter, Michael brought us a bouquet every day, while Lina visibly yearned after him. Then one afternoon Lina seized him by the arm and exclaimed, "Michael, you must tell them!"

"Tell us what, dear," I asked idly, admiring my new satin slippers.

"I know your secret, your highnesses," Michael said gravely, "but do not fear, I shall never tell anyone."

"Lina, how dare you...." I began, but he interrupted me.

"No, Princess," he said, "Lina told me nothing. A kindly magician gave me the power to become invisible, and I followed you a week ago, down the stairs, across the lake, and to the ballroom."

"Why are you telling us this?" I asked.

"Because, your highness, I have fallen in love with Lina."

"And we want to be married," Lina added breathlessly. Before I could speak, she rushed on. "And Papa said that whoever discovered our secret could marry whichever of us he chooses. And Michael has discovered our secret, and he chooses me."

"Neither of you is being quite sensible," I said. "Michael, if our secret is safe with you, as you said, how do you propose to marry Lina? You can't marry her unless you tell Father. And if you tell Father, there can be no more dancing. Additionally, dear," I added, as Lina appeared about to speak, "Father's thought was that one of us should marry a prince who might discover our secret. Supposing we were willing to let you divulge our secret, he would certainly not let you marry a mere gardener's helper. Lina, what can you be thinking of?"

"I thought," she stammered, "that perhaps if I told him how much I love Michael, Papa would ennoble him and then we could be married."

I stared pensively in a mirror, while all awaited my decision. After a while I said, "Well, I, for one, am becoming a bit bored with dancing all night, and would actually be willing to marry one of our princes and settle down. There is one with black hair and blue eyes who is particularly appealing.

"How say you, ladies, shall we permit Michael to tell Father our secret?"

At their nods, some more reluctant than others, I said, "Come Lina dear. You can but ask Father to ennoble your gardener's helper."

"Ennoble a gardener's helper!" Father roared. "Never! Oh, you may marry him if you wish, Lina. It is Lina? Yes, I thought so. I will even promote him to the position of full gardener. You may be a gardener's wife, if you are so silly. But I have a profusion of daughters for whom to find husbands, and I certainly shall not ennoble a gardener."

Do you know, she actually did it? She married Michael. We were surprised and saddened by this action, but as Father had said, there were many more of us. Since Father knew our secret, we disenchanted our princes, married our favorites, and sent the rest home with our apologies.

Naturally, since I am eldest, Father chose my prince to be his heir. He will, I am sure, prove to be quite as wise and just as Father, and with my help will be a good king.

I visit Lina occasionally in her gardener's tiny smokey cottage. It is very strange. She has five children, all boisterous boys, and has neither servants nor white bread, but she seems perfectly happy. I wonder how that can be?

...I see a midgety man approaching me with a jaunty walk and a smile.

The Brave Little Tailor

I'm walking down the road one sunny summer day when I see a midgety man approaching me with a jaunty walk and a smile.

"Seven at one blow!" he shouts at me.

I wonder what he means, but I see, when he comes closer, that he's wearing a sash around his middle which also says, "Seven at one blow."

"Seven what?" I ask him.

"I killed seven at one blow," he replied. "And now I'm off to see the world."

"Well, you're a fine little fellow indeed," say I. "Let's have a contest then, to see which is stronger."

"Splendid," he says.

So we sit ourselves down on a log, and I pick up a nearby rock nearly as big as the little fellow's head, squeeze it, and it crumbles in my hand.

"Match that," say I.

"Oh," he says, "nothing easier." Whereupon he plucks a piece of cheese from his bag, and squeezes it until the whey runs out. Well, he seems a pleasant little chap, so I pretend to believe he's squeezed a rock.

"My," I say, "that is a true feat of strength. Let's try another." I pick up another rock and hurl it out of sight across a hill, wondering how he will reply to this challenge.

And what does he do but take a bird from his bag and pretend to throw it! Of course, it flies high into the sky and disappears.

"Wonderful!" I exclaim. "Why don't you come home with me for a bite of supper?"

"Agreed," he says, and we go down the road to the cave where I live with some of my friends.

I expect him to be awed by the sight of several giants in a cave, but I am disappointed. Still as high-spirited as ever, he demands to know what's for supper. Well, my friends have been out raiding, and there are a few cows, a sheep, and a couple of hens.

"I'll have the sheep," I say. My friends have the cows, and the little fellow says he'd like a chicken or two. So we all eat merrily, and toss the bones into the fire, meanwhile telling stories of our prowess. If he's impressed by us, he doesn't show it, and when we've all bragged a bit I say to him, "Tell them what you've done."

"I killed seven at one blow," he says with a smile, which makes my friends uneasy.

When we decide it's time to sleep, I show the little man a bed where he might lie comfortably, while the rest roll up in our bearskins by the fire. When the others aren't looking, however, I give him a wink and a nod, telling him he should sleep elsewhere. He seems a clever chap, and may take the hint.

Sure enough, just before cock crow, Lob, one of my less kindly friends, rises from his bearskins, seizes the poker, and smashes it across the bed.

"That should do for seven-at-one-blow here," he says with satisfaction. I hope the tiny man has taken my hint.

Later, we all start out for our morning foraging, when who comes strolling out of the cave but my small friend. Well, this frightens Lob half out of his wits, thinking it's a ghost. He shrieks and runs off, which sets the others off, and soon only my tiny friend and I are left.

"Where are you off to now," I ask.

"To seek my fortune," he replies.

"Best of luck to you, then," say I, thinking that the tricky little man should do well for himself.

I hear later that he killed two giants, a raging bull, and a wild boar, and thus earned for himself the hand of the king's daughter and half a kingdom, but I wonder if that can be true, even for such a trickster.

I also wonder what in the world he killed seven of at one blow. Mice? Spiders? Flies?

There on my bed, sound asleep,
was a yellow-haired girl
about my age.

The
Three Bears

My name is Eddie Bear. Mother sometimes calls me "Baby," but that's for endearment. She calls Papa "Honey," too. We live on the edge of a forest, a perfect place for bird watching.

One morning, just after Mama had dished up our breakfast porridge, Papa spotted a yellow-footed fleacatcher perched in a nearby tree. This is a very rare bird, of course, so Papa grabbed the spotting scope, Mama grabbed the binoculars, and I grabbed the camera. We tiptoed out the back door to see if we cold get closer to the fleacatcher.

We returned about an hour later, having watched our quarry flit from tree to tree, listened to his lovely lilting song, and we hoped, taken some excellent pictures when he happened to alight on a branch in the sun.

The back door was standing open. Now I was the last one out, but I was sure I had pulled the door shut, very quietly so as not to scare the fleacatcher. We dithered awhile, wondering if there was a burglar still in the house, but finally Papa squared his shoulders and marched inside, followed more timorously by Mama and me.

What a scene greeted us! Papa's chair was moved out from its place, Mama's chair was moved out from its place and tipped over, and my chair was moved out from its place—and one leg was broken.

Papa's spoon was in his porridge dish, Mama's spoon was in her porridge dish, and my spoon was in my porridge dish—and the dish was empty!

We explored the other downstairs rooms, but it seemed that the intruder had come in the back door and not disturbed the rest of the house.

"My jewelry!" Mama suddenly exclaimed. "Do you suppose he's upstairs stealing my jewelry?"

Papa squared his shoulders again, picked up the broom for protection, and started up the stairs, followed by Mama and me. We went into Mama and Papa's room first. Papa's bed had been mussed up, Mama's bed had been mussed up, but there was no one in the room, and all Mama's jewelry was still in its box.

"My stereo!" I exclaimed. "Do you suppose he's in my room stealing my stereo?"

Papa squared his shoulders and marched into my room, followed by Mama and me. And there on my bed, sound asleep, was a yellow-haired girl about my age.

"So this is our thief and vandal!" Papa growled, which woke her up with a start. Seeing us grouped around the bed may have frightened her. Or perhaps it was Papa's broom. Anyway, she gave a little shriek, ran to the window, and jumped out. Silly thing.

We heard another shriek from down below, and when we went down to check, we found that she had broken her ankle. So we called her mother and father to tell them about the accident. Then we took her to the hospital, where they set her ankle and she was reunited with her parents.

But we never found out what she was doing in our house in the first place.

We went into the
house, where the mill
took pride of place, and he commanded
it to grind out gold pieces...

How the Sea Became Salt

My brother and I are so different that it is difficult to believe we had the same parents. It is not simply that he is very poor while I am rich, since we come alike from a poor family. But I am intelligent, ambitious, and quite ruthless, while he is intelligent but soft, giving away whatever meager means he manages to accumulate. He calls this sharing with those less fortunate. I call it foolishness.

One day he came to me, as he has many times in the past, imploring me to provide food for himself and his hungry family. And, as so often in the past, I gave him a ham and some bread, and bade him be more judicious in his "sharing." He assured me that he would, and that this would be the last time he asked for anything. I nodded and smiled, and calculated that it might be as much as a week before he was back begging.

When I had not seen him in over a month, I became curious and decided to pay him a visit to see what he was up to. Imagine my surprise at finding him and his family healthy and well-fed, and wearing fine clothes. His house was newly painted, the roof was patched, the garden prospering. The whole area exuded an air of prosperity. Now what, I wondered, has he managed to do right?

He seemed delighted to see me, and eager to explain. On his way home with the ham he had met an old woman who had implored him to share his food. Of course, my generous brother was only too happy to oblige. As he said, "The poor woman was so very hungry, and I had plenty." I make no comment on that kind of thinking.

After she had eaten her fill, the old woman said that my brother deserved a reward for his benevolence, and presented him with an antique hand mill. She then demonstrated its wondrous properties, which were that upon being given the correct command it would grind out anything desired. I would have been most dubious about such a story, had I not been able to see the obvious prosperity of my hitherto poverty-stricken brother.

I begged him to show me this marvel, which he was most willing to do. We went into the house, where the mill took pride of place, and he commanded it to grind out gold pieces. One has to believe the evidence of one's own eyes, and fingers (and teeth), and those gold pieces were as real as any I have seen.

After a short time he commanded the mill to stop. He explained that the command to stop was quite as important as that to start. This seemed odd to me, but he said that his wife, being hungry one day, had ordered the mill to grind herrings and broth and then forgotten how to stop it. The house was awash with broth before her cries reached my brother's ears and he gave the proper instructions.

I asked him to loan the mill to me, knowing that my loving brother would be only too happy to return some of my past kindnesses, and I was quite right. He ground out some food to put by, a new gown for his wife, a doll for his daughter, some toy soldiers for his son, and many more gold pieces. Then he said that I could borrow the mill for as long as I needed it, that he was happy to share it with me. For once I was pleased that he was so unselfish, and made my way to my home as fast as I could, hugging the mill protectively.

When I reached my home I had the mill turn out some gold pieces just for practice, in the meantime sending for a trustworthy sea captain in my employ. When he arrived I swore him to secrecy, demonstrated the working of the mill, and unfolded the plan I had made. When we were both sure he understood clearly, he took it with him and set sail.

Two weeks later I learned how all our plans foundered, together with my ship. He had put out to sea as instructed, but instead of having to sail a long distance to trade for salt, as in previous times, he sailed a few miles offshore in an empty ship. As soon as he was out of sight of land, he set up the mill, commanded it to grind salt, and proceeded to fill sack after sack with the precious commodity. The crew filled the hold with sacks, then stacked them on the deck, while the captain tried to recall the command for shutting off the flow. Of course, the more he tried to think of it, the less he was able, and meantime the salt piled up and the ship began to sink.

Instead of throwing the mill overboard and at least saving the ship, the pitiful fool stood on the deck issuing one useless command after another to the mill. The crew, having more common sense, launched the lifeboats, and dragged the captain into one as the ship sank from under him.

As to the mill, apparently it is still grinding salt, out there in the sea. Many fish are dying, and sailors report that the water is no longer fresh and fit to drink. Interesting. I wonder if there might not be a way to make a profit from that fact.

Ah, me, what it is be a large, cuddley animal!

Snow White and Rose Red

A greedy dwarf with magical powers is a fearful thing, as I found to my cost last year. I had just been betrothed to a lovely and intelligent princess from a neighboring kingdom. Unfortunately for me, I had celebrated my betrothal with too much wine, and had not guarded my tongue as is my usual wont. The upshot was that I boasted too loudly of my wealth, word of which reached the dwarf of whom I speak.

The next time I rode hunting into the forest, therefore, he contrived to separate me from my companions and changed me into a black bear. He then told my prime minister that I should be restored to my true shape only upon payment of a huge ransom of gold, pearls, and jewels. The prime minister paid him, but the dwarf laughed and said that I would be free of my bear's form only on his, the dwarf's, death.

Upon which I became a fiercely hunting bear, but not, I fear a successful one. That dwarf had more bolt holes than a tribe of rabbits. I had tried digging him out once or twice, but with no success.

As winter drew near I regretted somewhat that he had not changed me into a true bear, rather than simply giving me a bear's form. Because though I had no mind to hide away in a cave until spring, the cold was bitter, and food was hard to come by, while the cursed dwarf was snug and warm underground.

One night I chanced upon a small house, whose lights seemed to beckon, promising warmth, food, and companionship. I knocked awkwardly upon the door, which was opened by a pretty child who squeaked with fright at sight of me.

I assured her, as best I might in my growly voice, that I meant no harm, upon which her mother called to her to let me in. Trusting soul, she was, considering that it had been a day or two since my last unsatisfactory meal. Luckily for her I was still much too human to feel inclined to devour another human.

So I shook the snow from my coat and entered the cottage. There I found that the dark-haired little girl who had opened the door was sister to an equally pretty blonde child, both daughters to a comfortable and kindly widow. She bade them feed me, a most welcome bidding, and then permitted me to lie by the hearth and warm myself.

The girls, whose names I learned were Snow White and Rose Red, soon became quite comfortable with me, going so far as to roughhouse as if I were a large dog. They even had the impudence to beat me with hickory wands, which hurt not at all through my thick fur, but which I thought degrading. When I growled at them, however, they only laughed. Ah me, what it is to be a large, cuddly animal.

Thereafter, I spent each night stretched in front of the kindly widow's hearth, and the days hunting for the scarce game to supplement their larder. A boring existence, which taught me a deal of patience, especially with mischievous little girls.

I left in the spring, to hunt once more for the thieving dwarf. I had him trapped one morning, for he had been cutting wood, his wedge had slipped, and his long beard was caught when the log snapped shut. I was about to pounce upon him when I heard a familiar giggle and so hid in the bushes. Sure enough, up came my little friends of the winter, who inquired kindly of the dwarf what the matter was.

He snarled his story, and what did the kind-hearted little dears do but try to free him. When they could not pull the log apart to allow him to go, Snow White drew forth a tiny pair of scissors from her pocket and snipped off the end of the beard.

While I watched in frustration, the dwarf picked up a sack of my gold, snarled at the girls for ruining his beautiful beard, and was off down one of his infernal holes.

You may believe this or not, but the same sort of thing happened twice more. Once the dwarf was fishing, tangled his beard in the line, and was being pulled into the water by a very large trout, I rejoicing on the bank. But here came the girls, and freed him by cutting off some more of his beard, whereupon, grumbling, he took the bag of my pearls he had by him and popped down another hole.

The third time, a giant eagle had him in its talons when the girls wandered by. By dint of pulling, and yelling, and creating a great commotion, they managed to force the eagle to drop his prey, upon which the dwarf berated them for ruining his beautiful jacket. They seemed to find his ingratitude amusing rather than annoying, and ran off toward town laughing and singing.

But this time the dwarf overreached himself. The sun was shining brightly, and instead of popping down the nearest hole with his bag of my jewels, he laid them out upon a flat rock to admire their glitter. Because there was no cover nearby, there was no hope of sneaking up on him before he was out of reach again. I could feel my teeth chattering with my fury, but waited with what patience I could muster in the hope that something would distract him long enough for me to reach him.

And bless their hearts, here came Snow White and Rose Red, their errand in the town apparently completed, wending their way happily homeward. They were, for once, neither singing nor laughing, and were upon the dwarf before he had time to sweep the jewels into his bag. Much taken by the pretty baubles, they stopped to admire them. Since they were quite used to the dwarf's evil temper, they minded his scolding not at all, but exclaimed over this or that bright stone, while I crept up on the dwarf as silently as I could.

Rumor has it that the dwarf saw me, and begged me to spare him and eat the girls instead. A ridiculous story. Had he seen me he would have been down a hole in an instant, even, to save his miserable life, leaving the jewels behind. But he saw me not at all, and I killed him with one swipe of the mighty paw he had thoughtfully provided me.

As soon as he was dead, of course, I resumed my normal princely shape, and a time I had reassuring the girls that all was well. I rewarded them for their kindness to me with whatever jewels they liked best, and sent them home to their mother with an exciting tale to tell.

Upon my return to the palace, I employed a number of foresters to search out the dwarf's tunnels, and eventually my gold, pearls, and all other treasure were recovered.

I married my beautiful princess, who had waited patiently for my return, for she said she never doubted that I would eventually destroy the wicked dwarf.

As for Snow White and Rose Red, I saw to it that neither they nor their generous mother wanted for anything. When they were grown, Snow White married my head forester, and Rose Red wed my chief huntsman, and they, as I, have lived happily since.

The
Pied Piper

I don't get into Hamelin Town very often, since I am out in the fields with my sheep most of the time. Occasionally, however, I must go to town to barter for supplies.

I had noticed recently that the rats were becoming more than just a minor, and normal, nuisance. They were becoming a menace. They were everywhere, and absolutely fearless, all of which simply confirmed my notion that a town is no place for a man to live.

Last time I was there, however, when my son and I went into the inn for a bite of luncheon, there was a buzz of conversation in which I caught the word piper several times. Now I'm a piper myself. Well, a man has to occupy himself with something while minding sheep, he can't always be chasing wolves. So I was interested in this talk.

"They do say he claims he can rid the town of the rats," one said.

"I don't see how he can do that by piping," said another doubtfully.

"Well, what I say is," said the innkeeper, "if he can rid us of the vermin, I don't care how he does it."

"They say," remarked a prosperous-looking young man, "that the town Elders have promised him a large sum of money if he can exterminate the rats."

"I don't care what it costs," the innkeeper replied. "The rats eat up most of my profits anyway."

"Ah, but he do wear funny clothes," an old gaffer in the corner remarked. "Bright colors, my word. Never saw a man dressed so."

"Doesn't matter," the innkeeper said. "He could wear a ball gown for all of me, just so he does what he says he can."

All of this sounded so interesting that I decided to stay in town awhile to see what would happen. I sent my son home with our supplies, and with a message to my wife to mind the sheep for a day or two. She'd scold like a jaybird when I got home, but I thought it might be worth it.

Next morning early, I was awakened by a pipe played so beautifully that I felt ashamed of my own poor efforts. When I looked out the window I saw rats everywhere, all running as fast as they could toward the lovely sound of that piping. I was apprehensive about going out into the street, but I needn't have worried. The rats were so intent on following that pipe, they had no time to bother with mere people.

I followed the sound myself, and soon saw the piper, dressed in clothes of many bright colors. The rats were running at his heels, and he was headed for the river. Then I saw a sight which was so astounding that I'm sure it will remain with me to the end of my days. When he reached its bank, he stood quietly and piped away. And as fast as they could, the rats hurled themselves into the river, and were swept away by the current. Within an hour they were all gone. All of them! Not a rat to be found in the entire town.

When the last rat had cast himself into his watery grave, the piper turned and walked serenely toward the Town Hall, where the town Elders met him. Clearly they were pleased with his feat, and just as clearly they were troubled with something.

I edged closer, in time to hear the Mayor say, "Well, I know we agreed to pay you one hundred gold pieces, but...."

"And have I not rid your fair town of its rats, as I promised?" the piper asked quietly.

"Certainly," said another Elder, "but...but you didn't do anything. You just played your pipe."

"Oh? And could any of you have caused the rats to drown by 'just' playing a pipe?"

"No, of course not," replied a tall, thin Elder. "But we thought you would have to work harder to...."

"Yes," interrupted the Mayor, "and what about the pollution in the river? All those decaying bodies! They may even be a hazard to navigation, and we depend heavily on the river for shipping."

"And what do you propose to pay me, if not the hundred gold pieces as agreed?" the piper asked. He didn't raise his voice, but I thought I had never heard anything so frightening.

"Oh, pay him," I found myself thinking, "pay him before he does something dreadful."

But the Elders had other notions. "We suggest," the Mayor said, "that you accept forty gold pieces, and consider yourself well compensated."

"No, no, no," I thought, seeing the piper smile grimly. "Pay him, oh pay him!"

But, "Very well," he said, "give me the gold and I'll be on my way."

They had it all ready, in a bag, which the Mayor handed over with a flourish. The piper tucked it into his belt, smiled again, and put his pipe to his lips. He played a different melody this time, no less lovely, and began to walk toward the bridge over the river.

And behind him came—the children of Hamelin Town. From the crowd in the green, from the streets and houses they came, all the children, laughing and dancing to the music. Not into the river, but over the bridge and after the piper. Nothing anyone said to them moved them an inch out of their path. It was as if the adults had ceased to exist.

"This will never do," I thought, though I was grateful I had sent my son home. So I took out my own pipe, not to compete with the piper's tune, I could never do that, but to try what I could to remedy an awful situation. I blew the loudest, most discordant notes I could, notes which clashed horribly with those of the piper.

It succeeded. The attention of the children was distracted. They looked about them in the confusion as the piper stopped playing and turned to look at me. I thought I had never seen such fury in another's eyes, and wondered what he would do. He just stared at me, with the anger smoldering, as I pushed my way toward the Elders.

"Pay him!" I shouted, "Pay him what you promised, or by heaven I'll let him pipe your children away!"

Others, desperately clutching their children, took up the cry, while the piper looked on sardonically. After much foot shuffling and consultation, and dark looks at me and at the piper, they at last agreed. The Mayor sent a servant into the Town Hall to get the additional sixty gold pieces, gave it to the piper with ill grace, and he and the Elders swept into the Hall and out of sight.

The piper saluted me with his pipe and went on his way, while the townspeople crowded around me, thanking me and patting me until I felt like my daughter's worn-out rag doll.

"You must be our Mayor!" someone shouted, and others took up the cry.

"No," I said, "no. I'm a shepherd, I wouldn't live in Hamelin Town were you to pay me one hundred gold pieces."

And with that I hied me back to the peaceful countryside, my family, and my sheep.

'Oh Beast, my own Beast, do not die,'
I cried,
cradling his
head in my
lap.

Beauty and the Beast

My dear Sisters,

You have questioned repeatedly my decision not to marry the Prince, and at last the time has come to satisfy your curiosity.

You will recall that a little more than a year ago Father returned, depressed and discouraged, from an effort to salvage his fortunes. He stayed a night, you remember, in a mysteriously empty but strangely hospitable castle. In the morning, recollecting my desire for a single red rose, he plucked one from a bush in the garden, whereupon he was beset by a Beast of fearsome aspect.

You encouraged me to accompany Father when he returned to the castle as he had promised the Beast, for you blamed me for requesting the rose and causing the trouble. I will not dwell on the unseemliness of such a claim, in view of your own clamorous requests for jewels, gold, silks and satins.

Father has told you of our arrival at the castle, of our confrontation with the Beast, of the Beast's persuading him that I would not be harmed, and of our tearful farewell to one another.

That evening, after I had supped alone, and rather lavishly I might add, the Beast joined me and we talked of this and that. He seemed pleasant enough, though his appearance was frightening, and his voice a growl. I had just begun to become comfortable with him when he asked me to marry him. Shocked by his request, terrified of his response to a refusal, I nevertheless told him quaveringly that such a marriage could not be.

"Ah," he said, rising from his huge chair, "then I will bid you goodnight, Beauty."

Later I realized that his rough voice had held not anger, but sadness and regret, but my first reaction was astonishment at his name for me. It must be, I thought, that he is comparing me to his own appearance, for I had never, as you well know, been regarded as a beautiful woman.

I never saw the Beast during the day, but he came unfailingly every evening after supper. There was no lack of entertainment about the castle, which was splendidly kept though I never saw a servant. But I began to look forward to the Beast's visits, despite the fact that he ended each one by asking me to marry him. I became quite disturbed, he seemed so downcast each night when I refused him. I had forgotten, you see, how terrifyingly ugly I had found him when first we met. However, though I no longer found him unhandsome, I could not bring myself to accept his proposal.

The Beast had given me a mirror in which I could see what was occurring here in Father's house. After some months had passed, I was distressed to discover that Father was ill. I feared that he was worrying himself unnecessarily about my welfare. I begged the Beast for the privilege of a short visit with Father, to reassure him that I was well and not unhappy.

He granted my request reluctantly, insisting that I take the mirror with me so that I might see his face, and he mine.

"You must return in a week, Beauty, for my life depends now upon your kindness," he said. This I thought to be an exaggeration. Old tales to the contrary, I did not believe one might die of love.

As instructed, I closed my eyes and wished, and when I opened them I found myself in my old room here in Father's house, delighted to be here, and to see Father. He was equally pleased, and I thought you were also. All of you made over me, and my clothes, and my obvious good health, but I think now that only Father was sincere. For what reason could you have had for urging me, against my better judgment, to outstay my seven days? Did you hope that the Beast would be so angry when I finally returned that he would devour me?

You had been jealous of me for years, supposing that Father loved me best. I ought to have realized that you were jealous still, of my comfortable life and my fine jewels. Perhaps you were additionally irritated by the marriages you had rushed into in order to escape what you imagined to be poverty? I must admit, I was not favorably impressed by your husbands.

Whatever the reason, I had been home nine days when I at last *bethought me of the Beast's mirror. What was my horror to discover that he was very ill, that he was, in fact, dying. My fault! My Beast was dying, and it was my fault! How could I have been so cruel, so thoughtless? I knew then what I had not before, that I loved my Beast dearly, and that I wanted only to be with him.*

Grasping my magic mirror I closed my eyes and wished fervently to be back in my room in the castle, hoping desperately that my wish would be granted. It was. I had known from the image in the mirror that he was in the rose garden, and there I found him a few minutes later, weak and panting, clutching a red rose.

"O Beast, my own Beast, do not die, please do not die!" I cried, cradling his head in my lap. "I love you Beast, I have only now realized it, please forgive my foolishness, dear Beast. I will marry you, Beast, if you will but recover from this dreadful illness."

Whereupon there was a flash of brilliant green light, and I found myself cradling the head, not of my Beast, but of a handsome, perfectly healthy, total stranger. He was, he explained gravely when I demanded to know what he had done with my Beast, a prince who had been cursed into beast form by a wicked sorcerer. The enchantment could be lifted, he said, only when a maiden agreed, of her own free will, to marry him. I had done that and so we were now to return to his own kingdom to be wed.

But I could not. This man was certainly attractive, probably wealthy, possibly powerful. But he was not the beautiful Beast whom I loved. He was persuasive, charming, delightful. I was sure that we could be good friends. But I could not love him, and I certainly could not marry him.

Sorrowing for my Beast, I packed some clothes and sadly returned to Father's house. You are aware that the prince has sent letters and emissaries, and once visited in person, begging me to reconsider. I know that you have thought me incredibly stupid not to accept his offer. But my grief at the loss of my beloved Beast was too great. I have thought, nay I have hoped, that I might waste away as he did and thus end my anguish.

Fortunately, my hope was in vain. For he has come back! My handsome Beast has returned!

"Beauty," he growled in his warm, rough voice, "I find that I do not care to live without you. A kindly magician has restored me to my beastly form, my younger brother is only too happy to be the king's heir in my place, and I am here to take you back with me to our castle. Dear Beauty, will you come?"

And so you see, dear sisters, that though I refused the hand of the

Prince, I have made an even better match. He is waiting now for me to complete this letter, and then we shall be off to be married, and to live happily once again in his castle.

Do not concern yourselves further, I beg of you, about my welfare, or Father's. For he is going with us, to live out his years in comfort and in peace.

With Love,
Your sister Alisand

Some instinct caused me to peek out the
Window...

The
Three Little Pigs

When our mother died, my two younger brothers and I were left with a small legacy to divide among us. The family home, of course, came to me as eldest. Because it was spacious and comfortable, I encouraged my brothers to share it with me, but they preferred to take their inheritance, buy property, and build houses of their own. So I gave them my blessing and promised to visit them as soon as time permitted.

However, it was spring, and what with the planting and tending of the garden, it was more than a month before I had a chance to call on them. Additionally, I had to oversee the work of the two workpigs I had hired to point the bricks and paint the trim on the family home.

When at last, in mid-summer, I was able to stop by to see my youngest brother, I was surprised to find that he had built his house of bundles of straw.

"That seems a flimsy sort of a house," I said, looking around critically.

"It shelters me from the sun and will keep the rain and snow off in the winter. What more could I need?" he replied.

"Suit yourself," I said, "but it won't hold up in a wind storm."

He shrugged cheerfully, offered me a cup of tea, and we parted friends.

The next week I went to see my middle brother, and was surprised to find that he had built his house of bundles of sticks.

"That seems a flimsy sort of a house," I said, looking around critically.

"It shelters me from the sun and will keep the rain and snow off in the winter. What more could I need?" he replied.

"Suit yourself," I said, "but it won't hold up in a wind storm."

He shrugged cheerfully, offered me a cup of tea, and we parted friends.

It was late fall before I was able to see how my brothers were faring, what with getting in the harvest and preserving the bumper crop of apples we had that year.

When I came to my youngest brother's house, I was astonished to find that it had been blown completely flat. I hadn't been aware of a wind storm severe enough to do that much damage, but the family home was snug and tight so perhaps I hadn't noticed. I looked for my brother, but there was no sign of him. Thinking that he had taken refuge in my middle brother's house, I hurried there.

To my astonishment, the house of sticks was as flat as the straw house had been. I could not imagine why I hadn't noticed so turbulent a wind storm, or why, if both their houses were destroyed, they hadn't come to me for refuge. Perhaps they were afraid I would scold them for their foolishness.

Scratching my head, wondering where they had gone, I returned to my home. I worried about them all evening, and finally resolved to go to town next day to see if they were there.

Next morning, as I was preparing to set out, I heard a thunderous knock upon my front door. Thinking that it was my brothers, I was about to open the door, but some instinct, fortunately, caused me to peek out the window to see who was there. Imagine my astonishment and fright to discover an enormous wolf on the porch!

He soon tired of knocking and began to shout, "Little pig, little pig, let me come in!"

Well, there was only one possible answer to such a rude request. "No," I yelled back, "not by the hair of my chinny chin chin."

"Then I'll huff and I'll puff, and I'll blow your house in," he shrieked. And suddenly I knew what had happened to my poor brothers' houses, and to my poor brothers as well. Ah me, if only they had listened to my advice!

"Puff away, old wolf," I thought, as I heard him begin blowing. "This house is neither straw nor sticks. It won't blow down so easily."

Sure enough, after a time the wolf went away, panting and growling. When I heard him say that there was more than one way to catch a pig, I decided I had better be on my guard.

Thus when I heard, the following week, a gentle tapping on my door, I went to the window to see who it was before opening. It was the wolf.

This time he was smiling a treacherous smile, and said, in a voice I'm sure he meant to be wheedling, "Little pig, there's a fair in the town tomorrow. Won't you come with me? We could have such fun together."

I hadn't known about the fair, and I do love the excitement and the mouth-watering food, but I knew better than to come out of the house while the wolf was about.

"That sounds wonderful," I called, "what time shall we go?"

"If we went at noon we could have lunch at the fair," he coaxed.

"Agreed," said I.

Next day I arose early, hurried to the fair, where I had a delicious breakfast, bought a new shovel and some rope, and was home half-an-hour before the wolf came by.

"Noon!" I exclaimed through the door. "I thought you said dawn. I am so sorry, but I waited and when you didn't come I went on. I have been to the fair and returned."

He was enraged, naturally, so enraged that he jumped about and bit at his own tail. Then he made a mighty leap and landed on my roof. Silly creature! What could he have hoped to accomplish? I heard him prowling about up there, scratching on the tiles as if he would open a hole. He growled in frustration, pawing at the chimney. Perhaps he thought he could jump down into the fireplace. As if I would be so wasteful as to have a chimney large enough to admit a wolf. Why, all the heat would go up the flue and out of the house.

Just as I was wondering desperately if I was henceforth to be a prisoner in my own home, he jumped down. I saw that his attention was no longer on me or my house. It was focused, instead, on a lady wolf who was strolling by, probably on her way to the fair. As they trotted companionably out of sight I breathed a sigh of relief, hoping that together they would find someone else to harass. Apparently they did, for I never saw them again.

She held up her face so that he could kiss her.

Prince Hyacinth and the Dear Little Princess

$\mathcal{I}$am unfailingly astounded by the fact that a man will fall in love with a beautiful woman without having the least notion of what her character may be like, or whether her head is as empty as a barn in the springtime. It is a weakness to which princes and kings seem particularly liable.

Let me give you two examples, a father and son, both of whom fell in love with pretty faces. The father, the ruler of a small kingdom, had the misfortune to fall in love with a beautiful princess who was under an enchantment. Mine. He also had the intelligence to consult with a seer as to how to break the enchantment.

At that time I was posing as a splendid white cat at the princess's court, which enabled me to keep an unobtrusive eye on her while living in utmost luxury. The seer told the king, quite truthfully, that in order to break the enchantment he must step upon the tail of the princess's cat. I don't suppose I should be angry with the seer for revealing my secret, it was quite common knowledge in our group. He couldn't have known, nor could I, how agile the young king could be in pursuit of his goal.

The day he succeeded in treading on my tail, and heavily too, I might add, I changed to my rightful form and laid a curse upon him. He might marry his princess, I told him, but he would have a son who would never be happy until he found out that his nose was too long. I also explained that should he reveal what I had just said, he would die in dreadful agony.

He nearly laughed, I could see it, but his fear of me restrained him. I'm sure he wondered how a prince could fail to know that his nose was too long. Which shows that a king can be so isolated from his courtiers that he doesn't realize the extent to which they will flatter him. He would find out, I thought with satisfaction.

But he didn't. They had been married a year, and the queen was due to bear their first child, when the king was unfortunately killed in a hunting accident. He thus escaped my threat of a horrible death, and was spared the sight of his son's grotesquely huge nose.

The child's mother was naturally terribly upset by her baby's deformity, but her ladies in waiting assured her that all the world's best leaders had had large noses, and that such an enormous nose was surely indicative of such virtues as intelligence, wisdom, charm, and dazzling horsemanship.

Other courtiers took their cue from the ladies, and Prince Hyacinth, as they inappropriately named the child, grew to manhood being assured constantly that his was, in truth, a most magnificent nose, one to be imitated but never matched. I was about the court a great deal, in one form or another, and was endlessly entertained by the stories the courtiers invented to justify their admiration of the enormous beak which preceded the prince wherever he went.

When he was nearly twenty-one his mother, having decided it was time for him to think seriously of marriage, caused the portraits of several princesses to be brought to court. From these, he was to select his bride-to-be. Please note: he was to choose the woman with whom he would presumably spend the rest of his life merely on the basis of her pretty face.

I must concede that he exhibited the same faultless taste for beauty of feature as his father before him, falling hopelessly in love with the most attractive of the candidates for his approval.

Negotiations were soon concluded between Hyacinth's mother and the princess's father. Fortunately for Hyacinth, the father did not demand a reciprocal portrait.

But now Hyacinth's courtiers were faced with a problem, for the princess, who I admit was a beauty, had a small, rather pert little nose, and more than one obsequious fool was banished for making fun of it. They had become so accustomed, you see.

Finally one who was brighter than the rest hit upon a solution. (I must keep an eye on that young man, he may be useful one day.) Men, he said, and especially the leaders of men, should have large, commanding noses, fitting to their position. But women, being soft and gentle, are more beautiful if their noses are small, to go with their shrinking nature. A foolish notion, as I am sure he was aware, but it succeeded in satisfying Hyacinth.

The prince, by now quite besotted with his "dear little princess," was so impatient for their marriage that he set off to meet her as she was coming to his kingdom for the wedding. Now I had insisted that he would never be happy until he found out that his nose was too large. But I am not so flint-hearted that I wanted him to find out first from his precious princess's peals of laughter. So I appeared out of a bolt of lightning, and spirited his dear little princess away.

Well of course he was inconsolable, and determined that he would not return home until he had found her. I cannot imagine what his courtiers were thinking of to let him ride off into the forest by himself, searching for his lost love, but that is precisely what they did.

He wandered about until his horse was stumbling with exhaustion, and he was weak with hunger. Then I caused a cottage to appear in the distance, to which he naturally made his way. I greeted him at the door in the guise of an old woman. He explained that he was lost and hungry, and I assured him that I would be only too happy to give him supper and a bed for the night.

When he introduced himself, I exclaimed that I had known his father when I was a girl. I chattered on and on about my days at court, how popular and pretty I had been, how noted for my reticence, how all the courtiers had said repeatedly that I was quite the most restful girl they knew for I talked so little. I could see that poor Hyacinth was becoming quite exasperated. And hungry, since with all my talking I had never served him his promised supper.

I am sure he was thinking that I had been taken in by flattery, and that he was grateful that he had never been so fooled by his courtiers. At last I relented, gave him his meal, and showed him to a room where he could spend the night.

In the morning he rode away, still searching for his dear little princess. I followed, taking various appropriate forms.

Poor lad, he had been told all his life that his was a wonderfully handsome nose, but everywhere he went people laughed at it, which puzzled and irritated him, but did not cause him to realize that it really was too large.

By this time I was tired of Prince Hyacinth, tired of having his dear little princess on my hands, and anxious only to be rid of both of them. So I shut the princess up in a lovely crystal palace, where the prince had only to follow his nose to find her. He was wild with joy when he chanced upon her palace, and if she was shocked by his nose she was too well-bred to show it, or even to laugh, for which I was grateful.

Instead she held up her face so that he could kiss her. That was when he discerned that his nose was, in fact, not of a normal size, for he could not in any way bring his lips near to hers.

I'm afraid he said some rather naughty words when he made this discovery, but he did admit that the nose was too large, which was all I required.

I immediately changed it to one of normal size, and furthermore caused them to be transported instantly back to the place where I had abducted the dear little princess, from which point I presume that they returned in triumph to his court, celebrated their wedding, and lived happily ever after.

'You see,' he cried, 'See the beautiful jewels ... We are rich, rich!'

Hansel

and Gretel

I am a poor woodcutter, with a wife and two children to support on the meager coins I am able to earn. A few years ago there was a particularly hard winter, during which I was able to put away a bit of money.

But it was followed by a warm spring and summer, when no one needed firewood beyond that required for cooking. By fall, we had used most of our hard-earned coins, and were finding ourselves with less and less to eat.

Things were so desperate that at last my wife and I concluded that, young as they were, our children would have to go into the forest with us to help carry back the wood I cut.

Next morning we gave them each a bit of bread and bade them come with us. We went deep into the forest, built a small fire for the children, and told them to stay nearby while we gathered wood.

We spent the day collecting and bundling four faggots of wood, two of them smaller for the children to carry. When at last we brought the wood, with some difficulty I might add, to the place where we had left the children, they were gone. We called and hunted until well after dark, then gave it up and returned home, planning to begin another search at first light.

We got little sleep that night, as you may imagine, worrying about Hansel and Gretel alone in the woods, cold and frightened, perhaps threatened by wild animals. We arose early and were preparing to set out, when out of the forest came the children, looking tired, but safe.

With cries of joy we ran to embrace them. Then, because we had been so frightened for them, we began to scold.

"Where have you been, you naughty children?" my wife demanded. "Why did you not stay by the fire as we told you? We have been sick with worry all night long."

Gretel hung her head and wept, which won her a fierce hug from her mother. Hansel, however, drew himself up and shouted at us. "You meant to lose us in the forest. Do not try to pretend that you wanted our help, we know what you were about!"

"What!"

"I heard you, in the night, planning to lose us in the forest so that there would be enough food for you to eat."

My wife and I were so horrified by his accusations that we stood dumb, our mouths open, while he went on. "And do not pretend that we have been gone only one night. We have been in the clutches of a wicked witch for at least four weeks, and well you know it."

"Hansel," Gretel put in, timidly, but he roared on.

"We wandered for two days, hungry and tired and terrified, and then came upon a house all made from gingerbread and candy."

My wife felt his forehead and shook her head. No fever. What on earth could be the matter with the boy?

"The house," he said, "belonged to a witch, who put me in a cage to 'Fatten the boy up' as she put it. But I fooled her. Whenever she asked me to stick my finger through the bars, to see if I was fat enough yet, I stuck out a bone so that she thought I was still too thin."

"Tell them what happened next, Gretel."

Gretel shook her head, the tears streaming down her face.

"Very well then, I'll tell them. The witch decided it had been long enough, even if my fingers weren't fat. She built a fire in the oven, and told Gretel to climb in to see if it were hot enough yet. It's all right, Gretel," he added in a kindly tone, "I know you don't want to talk about it."

Gretel hid her face in her mother's shoulder, while Hansel continued his incredible tale. "Gretel," he said, "is a cunning girl, and claimed she didn't know how to climb into the oven. So the witch climbed in to show her—can you believe anyone could be so stupid? And then Gretel shoved her in and closed the door, and so the witch was burned up. And then Gretel let me out of the cage, didn't you, Gretel?"

Gretel shrugged helplessly and wept.

"Then we went into the witch's house, and found all kinds of jewels in a chest. I can see that you would rather not believe my story, but here is the proof!"

With a flourish, he thrust his hands into his pockets and poured out handfuls of little white pebbles. "You see," he cried, "see the beautiful jewels. Gretel has some too, in her apron pocket. We are rich, rich! Aren't we, Gretel?"

Sadly, Gretel emptied her apron pocket of pebbles. "Oh yes, Hansel, if you say so," she whispered.

"And we will share our wealth with you, Father and Mother, even though you tried to lose us in the forest. For we are kind and forgiving, aren't we, Gretel?"

"Yes, Hansel," she said again.

"He is quite mad, you know," my wife said to me quietly. And from the expression in his eyes, I greatly feared that she was right.

"The night in the forest must have driven him insane with fear," I said.

He is mad still, though usually quite gentle and biddable. He goes with me now to the forest to gather wood, and while he doesn't understand why we need work so hard, since we are wealthy, he makes but little difficulty. But I never trust him with an axe.

The Three Billy Goats Gruff

I don't eat people. Had a cousin once who ate them, said they were mighty tasty. But then they got angry at him and drove him out of the country. I like it here under my bridge, so I leave the people alone. I eat pigs, and sheep, and cows—and goats when I can get 'em.

There used to be a family of them living off over the hill yonder. Three brothers they were. Used to see 'em grazing, and wish they'd come down to the river to drink, but they stayed on their hill, mostly.

Then one day, while I was dozing, I heard trip-trap, trip-trap, the patter of hooves on the bridge over my head. Well! I popped up quicker'n a flicker to see if it was something edible. And it was, oh my yes, a tender little goat. One of those from up the hill, if my eyes didn't deceive me. Strayed off from his brothers, he had, just to make me a meal.

When he saw me, he gave a jump, but not far enough. I soon had him in my grasp.

"Oh, please don't eat me, Mr. Troll!" he begged. "Wait for my brother, who is bigger than I am. He's just coming."

That seemed sensible to me. Bigger is always better. So I let him go and went back under the bridge to hide. Pretty soon I heard trip-trap, trip-trap on the bridge, so up I popped and made a grab. He was bigger, too, oh my yes, a nice fat goat for my dinner.

"Oh, please don't eat me, Mr. Troll," he begged. "Wait for my brother, who is bigger than I am. He's just coming."

I was getting really hungry by then, and the thought of an even bigger goat was hard to resist, so I let him go, and went back to hiding.

Sure enough, pretty soon I heard trip-trap, trip-trap on the bridge, and popped up to seize the biggest goat. He had horns, of course, and because he was bigger than his brothers, his horns were bigger too. Really big, and sharp, and he was snorting and pointing them right at me.

Well, it wasn't as if I wasn't expecting something like that, was it? I knew he'd come charging at me. After all, he was the oldest and wisest of the three, and the others depended on him to protect them. Which only proves that goats aren't much cleverer than sheep, for I dodged those fearsome horns quite easily.

He made a delicious dinner, with some bones to gnaw on when I get hungry again. I'll leave his brothers alone until they get a bit fatter. They'll grow!

I wonder who started the story that trolls are slow-moving creatures? And what made a goat think that he could defeat a troll with nothing but a pair of horns and some hooves?

As she lay on the bank, the
lock of her Fairy Godmother's
hair fell in the stream...

The Goose Girl

When I was young, my mother persuaded the Queen to employ me as maid to the Princess. Mother, of course, thought this was a step up from living on the farm, and it was one less mouth to feed. If I felt confined by life at the palace, the Princess was undemanding, the work was easy, and I was not bitterly unhappy.

When the Princess was of an age to marry, her father arranged for a match between her and the Prince of a neighboring kingdom. Since the two kingdoms were not at war, it was deemed sufficient that I alone accompany Her Highness on horseback. We commenced our journey one fine spring morning. The Princess's fairy godmother had given the Princess a lock of her hair for protection, and a magical horse named Falada. I rode a small gray palfrey.

We had not traveled more than two hours when we came to a clear brook. Her Highness, being thirsty, begged me to get her some water, in her golden cup, forsooth. I was feeling cross, and told her to get it herself. You may believe me or not, but that is what she did, meeching, mewling, weakling as she was. Still later we approached a larger river, and she again begged me to get her a cup of water. By this time I was tired of her drooping and complaining, and told her again to get her own water. As she lay on the bank, dipping her cup in the water, the lock of her fairy godmother's hair fell into the stream and floated away, and with it her protection, poor dear.

We were much of a size, and she was a weak-willed girl. I, on the other hand, am strong, and knew what I wanted. So I took what I wanted. Her clothes, her horse, and her title. I compelled her to dress in my clothes and to act as my maid, threatening her with awful things if she did not obey me. She did, weeping.

I realized what a splendid plan I had had when we arrived at the palace of Her Highness's betrothed, who was a handsome lad, tall and charming, with dark eyes and black curling hair. As I dismounted from Falada, I casually requested that the King find some occupation for my maid, whom I would no longer need.

I did not, as rumor has it, have Falada killed, nor did the Princess have his head nailed over the gate to the city. What a grotesque notion! He was put in a stall in the King's stables, where he was treated with some kindness and not ridden too hard.

The King put the Princess to work as a goose girl, helping the goose boy with his job. A fitting livelihood, I felt. I, on the other hand, rather enjoyed the attentions of the handsome Prince, who turned out to be charming but dull, and very nearly as empty-headed as the Princess.

After a few days, the goose boy complained to the King that he could not work with the girl any more. She insisted on visiting the stables to talk to her horse, whom the boy swore was answering her. And she combed her hair instead of attending to the geese. When he begged to touch her hair, he said, she caused a wind to carry off his hat so that he was compelled to chase it, and by the time he returned it was done up again. It was clear to me that the poor oaf was suffering from unrequited love, together with a sense of mischief, but His Majesty chose to believe him.

I overheard him ask the Princess about the boy's accusations, upon which she wept, wrung her hands, exclaimed that she dare not tell him what the matter was, but then was quite easily persuaded to divulge my entire plot to his willing ears.

He, thinking to entrap me, dressed Her Highness in a sumptuous gown, and sat her across from me at table that evening. I pretended not to recognize her, and she in turn was gracious, smiling at me as if she were delighted to meet an amiable new friend. She didn't fool me for a minute.

After dinner, the King told her story as if it were a tale he had heard from a traveler. He didn't fool me either. Then he turned to me, thinking that I had not recognized Her Prissy Highness. He asked what the punishment should have been for the despicable maid. I realized that the game was up, but I pretended to give the matter serious thought.

"I believe, Your Majesty," I said judiciously, "that the maid should have been turned loose in a deep forest, to make her way as best she could."

"Aha!" His Fatuous Majesty cried, "and so it shall be! For the cruel maid is you, and the wronged Princess is..." he turned to the Dimpled Darling, "this lovely young lady!"

Stir of consternation throughout the dining hall. Joy in the eyes of the Prince, who no doubt had found me entirely too domineering. Then smiles all around, as His Majesty's court realized that they would have to deal with a simpering ninny rather than headstrong me.

I was given a gown of coarse cloth, the gray palfrey I had ridden, a cloak, and a bag of bread and cheese. As you can see, the King was not so ruthless as I. The King's guards accompanied me into the forest and left me, warning me not to return the way we had come. As if I would.

But I have always been much at home in the forest, and easily made my way into the neighboring kingdom, though not the one from which the Princess had come. There I caught the eye of a wealthy miller and married him. We have lived comfortably together for many years now, and our sons are learning their father's trade. I have no regrets.

Imagine my dismay....
I was to be placed
atop the glass hill.

The Princess on the Glass Hill

My name is Katrina, Princess Katrina. My very close friends are permitted to call me Katy. The gardener's son is one of these, but only when we are alone together.

You may wonder why the gardener's son has such a privilege, when all others must call me "Your Highness" or "Princess Katrina." It is very simple. We are in love. He is the handsomest man I have ever seen, tall and slim and strong, with dark curls and flashing black eyes.

His manners are not courtly, how could they be? He is the gardener's son. He brings me the most beautiful flowers and we contrive to have conversations on many topics. Unlike the usual vacant-headed courtier, he is knowledgeable, intelligent, and amusing. A truly gentle man. I love him dearly.

You may imagine my dismay, then, when my father announced that it was past time I was married, and that there would be a contest for my hand. I was to be placed atop the glass hill which is near the palace, and whichever noble or knight was able to retrieve the three golden apples I would hold, should have my hand.

"Do not be distressed, Katy," Conrad said when he heard the news. "There is an opportunity in every problem, if only one is willing to search deeply. Believe me, you may sit serenely on the glass hill and enjoy the view."

The first day of the contest, many knights and nobles tried in vain to ride to the top of the hill, where I sat enthroned, as serene as I could contrive to be, with the apples in my lap.

None were able to ride higher than a step or two before they slid back to the bottom, until late in the afternoon. Then there came a knight clad in copper armor, who rode a third of the way to the top. I felt that such an impressive effort should be rewarded, so threw him one of the apples. He caught it, waved jauntily, and rode away without disclosing his identity.

The second day, while all the others failed, a knight in silver armor rode two-thirds of the way to the top. Because of the way he sat his saddle, I was sure it was the same knight, so I threw him the second apple. Again he rode away.

The third day he came again, this time wearing gold armor. He rode all the way to the top, seized the apple from my hand, and rode off.

Very mysterious. Someone had fulfilled the conditions, but no one knew who it was. Father sent messengers throughout the kingdom, requiring everyone's attendance in the square in front of the palace, so that the identity of the mysterious rider might be determined.

When the crowd was largely assembled, with my father and I seated upon thrones near the palace portal, and no one had admitted to having the apples, my perplexed father scratched his head and wondered aloud what to do next. A sudden murmur in the multitude caused us to look off to the north, and there was the golden knight on his prancing steed. The crowd moved aside to permit him to approach the thrones.

"I have the golden apples," he announced, as he drew near, "and here they are." He handed them gravely to Father, who looked on him with admiration and approval. "I claim your daughter's hand," he continued, "and half the kingdom."

Half the kingdom, forsooth! That had not been part of the promise. Kings do not give halves of their kingdoms with their daughters' hands, else kingdoms would eventually become as small as small estates. My Conrad would never have been so foolish.

Nor could I have considered marriage to a knight who was so silly as to wear copper, silver, or golden armor. Armor is intended for protection during battle, and for that only steel has the necessary strength.

I stood up. "I will not marry this knight, however noble he may be."

"My dear daughter," Father protested, "he has fulfilled the requirements perfectly. You surely cannot expect me to break my word."

"Certainly not, Father," I replied, "but he has not brought you the golden apples."

"What!"

The glittering knight drew himself up. "Do you dare to suggest that I have deceived your father," he demanded.

"Of course not," I said. Serenely. "However, the apples you have won are not the true golden apples. They are gilded lead."

"Nonsense," Father said, drawing his knife. "My word," he said, as he scraped away the gilt which covered a leaden apple. "But then...where are the true golden apples?"

"I have them," Conrad called from the back of the crowd. He held them up as he made his way to the throne.

"But how did you...?" Father sputtered.

"It was really very simple, Your Majesty," Conrad smiled. "You had proclaimed that Katy's, er, Princess Katrina's hand should be given in marriage to the person who retrieved the golden apples." I'm afraid I smirked. A very unprincessly thing to do, but I couldn't help myself.

"Well yes," Father said, glaring at me repressively. "But..."

"I realized," Conrad went on, "that I could never hope to ride to the top of that slippery hill. Somehow, though, the Princess was able to get up there, and if she could, I could. So I searched until I found the secret door at the back of the base of the hill, went up the spiral staircase to the top, 'retrieved' the apples from Her Highness, and replaced them with the leaden ones this bold knight has given you."

Father looked both disgusted and interested as he peered at Conrad. "I've seen you about the palace, have I not," he asked. "Your face is familiar."

Conrad swept him a rather awkward bow. "I am the gardener's son," he said.

"The gardener's son!" exclaimed the golden knight. "He is of common stock, sire. You surely cannot mean to permit your only daughter to marry one who is not noble."

"Oh well, as to that," Father said, "if Katy wants to marry him... Do you want to marry him?"

"Oh yes, Father, for I love him with all my heart."

"Well then, nothing simpler," said Father, drawing his sword. "Come here, boy. Kneel before me."

Conrad approached apprehensively, while I reassured him with a smile.

Father touched his shoulder lightly with his sword, proclaiming, "I hereby name thee Duke Conrad. There, you see," he turned to the glittering, frustrated knight. "Now she may marry him if she wishes. It is no very bad thing for a princess to wed a duke, after all."

A short time later we celebrated a double wedding—I to my Duke Conrad, and the golden knight to a neighboring princess, a friend of mine, who was impressed by his lustrous armor and courtly manners.

I saw a motionless white figure standing next to me.

The Girl Who Set Out to Learn About Fear

My elder brother is far more intelligent than I, but one day I will be a queen, while he will never be more than a prosperous farmer. Here is how this came about.

My brother, who in all other things excelled, feared to walk through a graveyard after dark. He said it made him shudder. When I asked him what he meant by that, I got a disgusted look but no answer. I even walked through the graveyard several times at night, but to no effect.

I also noticed that when friends came to visit, they sat about the fire and told stories, which they claimed were frightening, and made them shudder. I never could see why, nor what they meant by shuddering, though I asked repeatedly.

At last one day the sexton overheard me exclaim, "Oh, if I could only learn to shudder," and he kindly offered to teach me.

"Come live with me and my wife awhile, and ring the church bell for me," he said. "In return, I'll teach you to shudder."

I was delighted, and my father, who had tired of my plaint about shuddering, was pleased to be rid of me for a time.

So the sexton showed me how to ring the bell. I had been at the job for several days, and was disappointed not to have learned to shudder, when the sexton woke me one night.

"Come," he said, "you must ring the bell right now."

I didn't understand why the bell should be rung in the night, but went with him willingly enough. We climbed to the top of the belfry, and I was about to begin to ring, when I saw a motionless white figure standing near me.

I inquired politely who it was, but it gave no response. "You must move out of my way," I said, "for I cannot ring the bell with you standing there."

Still nothing. "I will warn you one more time," I said, "and then I must make you move." Nothing.

Now I'm a big strong girl, and I was provoked. So I grasped the figure and threw it down the stairs, then rang the bell and went back to my bed.

Next morning, the sexton's wife asked me if I had seen the sexton, who had not returned to his bed after rousing me to ring the bell.

"No, ma'am, I've seen no one but a white figure who got in my way when I wanted to ring the bell. So I pushed it down the stairs."

Well, it was the sexton, and the poor man's leg was broken. I couldn't imagine why he had stood there all clothed in white and said not a word, nor did I understand why both he and his wife were so angry with me. But they were, and sent me home immediately. And I hadn't learned to shudder as he said I would, either.

My father was angry, too. "You great ninny," he shouted, "what am I to do with you?"

"I'm sure if I could learn to shudder, I could make my way in the world," I replied.

"You cannot earn your way by shuddering, you foolish girl."

"Nevertheless, Father, that is what I should like to do. I'm sure if I could learn to shudder everything would be just fine. Oh please, Father, let me try."

"Very well girl," he said at last, "but you must wear some of your brother's old clothes. I cannot send a maiden out alone to earn her way." He went to the chest in the corner and took out a bag. "Here are fifty silver pieces," he said. "And I hope you are successful in your absurd quest. Come home when you run out of money."

So I dressed in my brother's clothes and set out to learn to shudder. I walked along and walked along, and presently came to an inn, where I decided to stay for the night. During a hearty supper, I told the innkeeper that I had set out to learn to shudder.

"Oho," he said, "I have just the thing for you. There's a haunted castle nearby, and the king has offered a large reward to anyone who can stay three nights in it."

"You must understand," his wife added, "that many have gone in but no one has ever come out. You're a pretty lad. Won't you reconsider?"

"No," I said, "for I really wish to learn to shudder."

Next day I went to the king, and received his permission to stay in the haunted castle, though he, too, tried to discourage me. So I collected some food and some firewood, went into the castle, built a fire in the fireplace, and laid myself down to sleep.

When the king came to the castle, after the third night, he seemed surprised to find me still alive, I can't think why. There had been some disturbances, true enough, but nothing very serious. And I still hadn't learned to shudder.

He exclaimed that I had broken the enchantment on the castle, and that in addition to an immense reward, I was to have his daughter's hand in marriage.

"That won't do at all," I said, "for I am a girl, and cannot marry your daughter. Furthermore, I haven't learned to shudder, though that's what I set out to do."

Just then a young man spoke up. "I will marry her, Father," he said.

"You cannot marry a nobody," the king said.

"But you were willing that my sister marry this nobody," the young man replied.

"Yes, but you are the heir to the throne."

"I know, and my sister is only a princess. Nevertheless, I will marry this nobody and none other."

"But why?" the king asked.

"Because she is courageous, and pretty, and more interesting than any girl I have ever met."

By this time I was goggling. "Is no one going to ask me what I want?" I inquired. "Because I didn't come here to be married. I came to learn to shudder, and I haven't learned yet."

The prince took my hand. "Marry me, you bewitching creature, and I promise I'll teach you to shudder," he smiled.

He was very handsome, and seemed kind, so I agreed, and we were wed with great pomp. My father and brother came to the wedding, and pretended to be glad for me.

We had been married a month, during which time I had repeatedly begged my husband to teach me to shudder. He always told me to be patient, that he was waiting for just the right circumstances.

Finally one morning, when the frost coated the last leaves of fall, and there was a skim of ice on the pond, he said the time had come.

"You must take off your dress and shoes," he said, "and climb into this tub in your shift." I must have looked doubtful, for he took my hand and begged me to trust him.

I did as he said, and then he told me to shut my eyes. I heard a sloshing sound, and suddenly a bucket of cold water filled with tiny minnows, was dumped over me.

And I shuddered, oh how I shuddered!

He laughed as he lifted me from the tub and wrapped a warm blanket around me. "Now you have learned to shudder, dear wife," he said. "Do you like it?"

"No, I do not," I replied, draining the water out of one ear and then the other. "But I have learned another important lesson, too."

"And what might that be?"

"I've learned never to climb into a tub in my shift, and shut my eyes."

He dropped the baby in the river, sure that he had defeated Fate.

The Fish and the Ring

When my brother Leon, a powerful baron, declined to recognize my husband, on the grounds that my dear Jack is of common birth, I determined to gain revenge. Since Leon is a magician, as are many of our family, I decided to become Fate to his Seer. He would look into a Book of Fate as planned by me.

Therefore when Leon's son Peregrine was a lad of about four years, the apple of his father's eye, Leon forecast the boy's future, and saw that which horrified him. His son, Fate decreed, would marry a low-born maiden.

This was not a thing to which he could agree, so he looked further into his Book to see if the maiden had yet been born. She had, to a poor family with far too many mouths to feed. So he set off to remedy the situation by paying the poor family a goodly sum for the child, telling them that the lass would be a companion to his son.

As soon as he was out of sight, however, he dropped the baby into the river, and went away sure that he had defeated Fate.

"Ah, Leon," thought I, "you are not the only one with magical powers. I am now this child's Fate, and it shall not be as you desire."

So I kept her afloat until she was found by a childless couple who were delighted to have such a lovely little girl so wonderfully bestowed upon them.

Thereafter I paid little attention to the girl, whom her foster- parents had named Sylvia, other than to make sure she was growing properly, until one day when Leon and his friends went hunting near her home. Aha, thought I, I must watch to see how this develops. Sylvia was by then a well-mannered young woman, who impressed the baron's companions with her beauty.

One of them expressed the belief that such an enchanting child was sure to marry well, and suggested that Leon tell her future. He grumbled, but agreed, and was appalled to discover that this was the very lass he had cast into the river years before. He much feared that Fate would prove stronger than he, but persevered in his efforts to defeat it.

"Your parents are poor and in need of assistance, I see," he said to Sylvia, pretending of course that he didn't know her history. "You are a pleasant child, and so I will help you to better their condition. Take this note to my brother, who will give you work to do and a wage to send home to your father and mother."

Sylvia, being a dutiful child, bade her foster parents a tearful farewell, and set off for our brother Matthew's castle. Now the note said, "You must ask no questions, but put the bearer of this note to death immediately. She is a grave danger to our family."

I couldn't approve of that, of course, and so while she spent a night at a small inn, I substituted a note which said, "You must ask no questions, but marry the bearer of this note to my son immediately."

Matthew was puzzled to receive such a message, but as he was much younger and accustomed to following Leon's orders, he arranged the wedding for the day after Sylvia's arrival at his castle. And wasn't it wonderfully fortuitous that Peregrine was visiting at Matthew's castle just at the time when the lass arrived there?

They were both attractive young people, and very much taken with one another. He, of course, had always known that his father would select his wife for him, while she felt greatly honored to be marrying such a grand young gentleman. But they were not to live happily quite yet, for Leon was not done with trying to outwit Fate.

When he heard of the marriage he pretended to be pleased, all affability when he went to visit Matthew and the newly-married couple. Then he tried once again to overcome Fate. He invited Sylvia to walk with him, and as they came to the edge of a cliff over the sea he seized her and would have thrown her into the waves.

When she begged to know why he wanted to kill her, he told her that he could not countenance a marriage between his high-born son and a common maiden. She was puzzled, since his note had specified that they were to be married. However, she was clever as well as beautiful.

"Spare my life," she begged, "for I am not at fault. It was Fate. But I will promise never to see you or your son again unless you desire it."

He was apprehensive lest the sea spare her life, as he supposed the river had. So he thought of another plan. Taking off his gold ring, he hurled it into the water.

"You may claim my son for a husband when you are able to show me that ring," he said. "Until then, do not let me see your face."

She went wandering for many a weary mile until she came upon the castle of a kindly earl, who gave her work in his kitchen. Meanwhile, I was racking my brain, trying to devise a plan whereby Sylvia could come upon Leon's ring.

Now her foster father had been a fisherman, and her foster mother had taught Sylvia many a delicious way to prepare fish for the table, which at last inspired the plan which finally defeated Leon's efforts to circumvent Fate.

I caused a large fish to swallow Leon's ring, a fisherman in the employ of the earl to catch the fish, and the earl's chief cook to consign the preparation of the fish to Sylvia—and all of this at a time when Leon and Peregrine were visiting the earl.

And so of course she found the ring and slipped it into her pocket. Then she baked and seasoned the fish so perfectly that the dinner guests insisted on congratulating the cook in person.

When she came into the dining hall, Peregrine, who had been grieving for her, was delighted. Leon was furious, but she slipped the ring on her thumb and held it up for him to see. I'm afraid her grin was a bit triumphant, but who can blame the child, after all she had been through?

Then at last, Leon had to admit that Fate was stronger than he. He took her hand, and turned to the assembled guests. "This is my son's wife, who has been lost and is found," he said, while Sylvia and Peregrine looked soulfully into one another's eyes.

Since that day I have found, to my pleasure, that Leon looks more benignly upon my beloved, low-born Jack.

She was wearing a tiny mask over her eyes, to match the loveliest gown I had ever seen.

Cinderella

Tales about wicked stepmothers weary me, since although I am a stepmother, I am in fact not wicked at all. I am sure Elinor would agree with me entirely.

Her actual name is Elinor, you know. Somehow the ridiculous nickname of Cinderella has become attached to her, as the "wicked" appellation has to me, and neither is true. Furthermore, I cannot feel that Princess Cinderella sounds as well as Princess Elinor.

Let me tell you the true tale, and you may decide for yourself what manner of stepmother I have been. When I married Elinor's father he had been widowed for just over a year, and I for three.

Elinor was a shy slip of a girl, fifteen years of age and just over five feet tall. Tiny and forlorn, she was, poor little thing, trying to keep up the house in her mother's place with no help from her father, who is at best indifferent to creature comforts. When my daughters Mathilde and Clothilde and I moved into the house that spring, we naturally began to take up the chore of running the large house.

How do the rumors start? It is not at all true that we made Elinor do all the housework, while we primped and preened. Nor did we compel her to sit in the ashes by the fireplace. She spent a great deal of time curled up on the hearth, it is true, not because we forced her to do so but because she was cold. The little creature hadn't enough flesh on her bones to keep her warm.

So we went on very amicably for a year, the three girls and I, keeping a comfortable house for Claude while he conducted his successful mercantile business.

Just after Elinor's sixteenth birthday, and a grand celebration we had too, Claude coming out of his preoccupation long enough to present her with a doll, we received invitations to three festive balls the Prince proposed to give.

Such excitement! All the young ladies and gentlemen in the realm were invited, as well as some older ones to act as chaperons. Mathilde, Clothilde and Elinor were wildly enthusiastic, of course, and I determined that I would attend as chaperon, even in the face of Claude's indifference.

It occurred to Elinor, perhaps unfortunately, that she ought to ask her father's permission to go to the ball. The result of her request astonished me.

"No," he said adamantly, "she is too young."

"Claude!" I exclaimed. "She is sixteen. Surely that is old enough to begin to..."

"Enough!" he said. "Look at her, she is but a child. She may not go, and that is my final word on the matter."

We all knew by now that to argue with Claude when he had made up his mind was futile, but I can tell you that I was furious. Elinor, who understood her father better even than I, was wistful and unhappy, but because she is a kind and unselfish girl, she willingly helped my daughters and me to sew lavish ball gowns. Despite his abstraction, Claude was a generous provider, and begrudged us nothing we desired.

When the night of the first ball finally arrived, Mathilde, Clothilde and I boarded Claude's best carriage in a state of high excitement. Poor Elinor's eyes were swimming with tears as we dressed, and since I was sure there would be more than enough chaperons I offered to stay home with her.

"No," she said bravely, "there is no sense in your missing the fun just because Papa does not know that I am no longer a child. You go, have a splendid time, and tell me all about it when you return."

A thoroughly nice girl. How can anyone suppose that I was cruel to her? In the year we had been together, I had come to love her dearly.

The music at the ball was delightful, the gowns of the ladies were colorfully lovely, the refreshments were all that could be desired. We had a marvelous time. The Prince was kind enough to dance with each young lady, including my daughters, who were thrilled to be so honored. But after the unknown beauty arrived, the Prince danced only with her, and who could blame him?

The lies people tell! They say that we did not recognize Elinor because she was always covered with ashes at home, or that we had never really looked at her. Idiotic. She was a little beauty and we all knew it. We did not recognize the unknown belle for a perfectly simple reason: She was wearing a tiny mask over her eyes, to match the loveliest gown I had ever seen. We might have suspected because of her size, but how could we be expected to know that she had a fairy godmother, or that she would dare to circumvent her father's orders?

She was at home when we returned, and seemed delighted to hear all the details we could call to mind about the ball, and of the beauty who appeared to have stolen the Prince's heart. She even speculated with us as to whether the beauty would appear at the second and third balls. She has since explained that she wasn't herself sure that she would be permitted to go.

The second ball was much like the first, except that the Prince, though he danced with others early in the evening, had eyes for no one but the unknown young lady once she appeared. He was, we explained later to Elinor, entirely smitten.

My girls, by the way, met on the second evening the two young merchants' sons whom they subsequently married.

At the third ball the beauty was even more lavishly gowned than at the previous ones, with, if you can credit it, glass slippers upon her feet. The Prince danced with no one until she arrived, and had eyes for her alone the entire evening, at least until midnight when she dashed hurriedly away, as she had done each night. When we told Elinor about this, she said wistfully that perhaps the beauty's father was as strict as her own.

Three days later, with much fanfare, the Prince came to our town. He was, his crier announced, attempting to find the owner of a glass slipper dropped by the unknown beauty the night of the third ball. All young ladies who had attended the ball were to try the slipper.

Have you heard the ghastly tale of how my girls took a butcher knife and cut off their toes and heels in a futile effort to make the slipper fit them? Where do these stories start? Of course, they did no such thing. In fact, they laughed themselves silly when the Prince's courtier insisted they try the tiny slipper. They are tall girls, with feet in accordance with their height, and neither could get more than a big toe into the slipper.

The Prince and his courtier were about to take their leave when Elinor asked shyly if she might try. She and Mathilde had been outside hanging out laundry when the Prince came into town, Elinor's hair was still wind-blown, and she was wearing an old gown suitable for housework. She resembled not at all the lovely young girl who had stolen the Prince's heart.

Clothilde started to say that Elinor hadn't been at the ball, but subsided when I hushed her. There was something in Elinor's demeanor which told me to let her try the slipper. It fit, of course, and when the

Prince looked somewhat doubtful, she drew a matching slipper from her pocket, to his ecstatic delight.

Before they were married, she told us the entire tale of her attendance at the ball. Will you believe that her own father was as astounded as the rest of us. He had totally forgotten that the poor child had a fairy godmother.

So Elinor has wed her Prince, my girls have married their budding merchants, and all are likely to live quite happily for many years.

A third outlaw spoke up.
"Fear, my boy, is
wherever We are!"

The Boy Who Found Fear at Last

*I*lived with my mother at the edge of a forest for the first several years of my life. Mother never could remember for sure how old I was, but the incident that changed my life must have occurred when I was about eighteen. It was a stormy evening, and a gust of wind suddenly blew the door open.

Mother shivered. "Oh, I feel so frightened," she said. "Go shut the door quickly, son."

"What is it like, to feel frightened?" I asked.

"Well, it feels like being, um, frightened," she explained.

"You couldn't be a little clearer, could you, Mother?"

"No I can't," she snapped, "but once you get out into the world I daresay you'll discover what I mean soon enough."

Not many months later my mother took a raging fever and died. Since there was nothing to keep me in our tiny cottage, I set off to see the world. And to discover, if I could, how it felt to be frightened.

I had traveled several days, not having any very clear goal, and found myself one evening deep in a forest. Spying a light just off the path I made for it, hoping for companionship and perhaps a bite to eat.

The light was made by a fire, around which sat a rough-looking group of men. Finding a gap in the circle of men, I made my way to the fire to warm my hands.

"Ho!" one of them said, "who are you and what do you imagine you're doing?"

"My name is Dominic," I replied, "and I am making my way in the world. Will you share your meal with me? I haven't any money to pay, I'm sorry to say. Your fire is wonderfully warm."

"Here you are, in the midst of a fierce group of outlaws, boy, and you beg for food? Anyone else would be frightened to death," said another of the men.

"There!" I said. "That's another thing. Not long before she died, my mother was frightened. She said that when I got out into the world, I would learn what fear was, but I haven't found it yet."

A third outlaw spoke up. "Fear, my boy, is wherever we are."

"Where?"

"Right here with us!" said another.

"I don't see it anywhere."

"Fear is not something you can see, it's something you feel," the first one said.

"Oh. Well, I don't feel anything, but I am hungry. If you will give me a bite to eat, I'll continue my search in the morning."

"Ah, but if it's fear you're looking for, we'll teach you that. Just you take this pan and some flour and sugar and butter to the graveyard that is just down the road. There you shall bake us a cake for our supper. You'll find fear there, I feel sure of it. We'll give you a bite to eat when you return—if you return."

Well, I took the pan, flour, sugar and butter, and went as they directed to the graveyard. There I built a fire of my own, stirred up the ingredients, and propped the pan over the fire to bake. Just as I took it off the fire, a bony hand reached up from the nearest grave, and a voice demanded that I share the cake.

Well, I wasn't going to have that, was I? The cake was for the outlaws, with perhaps some for me. So I rapped the hand across the knuckles with my spoon, put out the fire, and returned to the outlaws.

"Well," demanded one of them, "have you found fear?"

"No," I said, "was it there? I must have missed it somehow. A hand reached out for some cake, but I didn't think you'd want me to share it, so I refused."

The outlaws looked at each other strangely, I thought, but they kindly shared their supper with me. Next morning, one of them said that if I would go across the mountain, toward the rising sun, I would come to a deep pool where I would be sure to find fear. As you may guess, I went eagerly.

Toward evening I came to the pool the outlaw had described. Next to the pool was a tall tree with a swing in it, and a little boy in the swing. Nearby was a young girl, crying bitterly. When I asked what was wrong, she said she wanted to take her brother from the swing but couldn't reach it. If I would allow her to stand upon my shoulders, perhaps she would succeed.

I didn't mind, and knelt down so she could climb on. But instead of lifting the boy from the swing she pressed down on my shoulders so firmly that I thought I might fall into the pool. So I gave a heave and threw the girl behind me.

I turned to look for the boy in the swing, but he had disappeared, and when I turned back to the girl to demand an explanation, she too had disappeared. This was all very mystifying, but since I still hadn't found fear, I decided to continue my search.

I wandered for months, meeting many folk who said they would show me fear, and many others who claimed to feel fear, but never once did I understand what they were talking about. I had begun to despair of ever finding it myself.

At last one day I came over the crest of a hill and spied a large city in the distance. Here, if anywhere, I thought, there will be someone who can teach me what fear is. I began to whistle, thinking that my quest would at last be successful.

The streets were so full of people I could hardly make my way, but at last I found myself in a large square. All these people were looking up at the top of a tower, shading their eyes and craning their necks.

"What is everyone looking at?" I asked a man standing near me.

He looked at me as if I were the most ignorant person in the world. Well, I suppose I was.

"The king of this country has died and left no heir," he finally explained. "At noon a dove will be released, and the new king will be the person it flies to."

Though it seemed strange to me, I supposed that was as good a way as any to select a ruler. I'd have thought that a man's ability to rule and make wise judgments would be most important, but thought perhaps they bred a particularly discerning kind of dove in this land.

When the sun was high over head, and the bells began to toll their twelve notes, a door at the top of the tower opened, and a dove flew out. It flew about for a minute or two, then came and landed on my shoulder.

"The king, the king!" people shouted, "This man is our new king!"

I thought of the decisions a monarch must make, of his power of life and death over his subjects, of the need to better the conditions of the poor, to make miserable people happy, to punish the wicked, of never being able to do as he wished, nor even marry for love.

"No, no!" I howled. "There has been a terrible mistake, I cannot be your king, I am only a poor peasant."

Someone in the tower released three more doves, to make very sure the right person had been chosen, and they all flew straight to me. A strange shiver ran down my back, which I was at a loss to explain. Then suddenly I realized what it was. I had at last found what I had sought for so long a time. Fear.

That was many years ago, and I have ruled as best I might for all that time, and in all that time I have never been free of my fear of being a bad king.

When my husband came in, he sniffed suspiciously.

Jack and the Beanstalk

I'm a giant. So's my husband, Coll. You're surprised that there are female giants? Did you really suppose giants married little people like you? Nonsense. Why would they? The temptation to eat you would be overwhelming.

We have gigantic appetites, appropriate to our size. That's why people don't like us. We eat their cows and sheep and goats and pigs. Rabbits and chickens we leave alone—too small to bother with. But there's nothing like a change, and the most delicious change is man flesh.

That's why we were rather pleased when my cousin stole the beans. We were sure he'd sell them to some poor soul, who'd soon come climbing up the beanstalk and provide us with a meal. We looked forward to that.

And sure enough, not more than a week later, here came a strange boy begging food. So I gave him a bit of porridge, and kept him talking until I heard Coll's footsteps approaching. Then I feigned panic, and urged the boy, who had said his name was Jack, to hide in the oven. Later, I would build up a fire, and cook him for our supper.

When my husband came in, with a lovely cow for our lunch, he sniffed suspiciously.

"I smell a strange man," quoth he.

"Oh no, my dear, that can't be," I replied, winking and pointing at the oven.

"Oh well, perhaps you're right," he grinned, and helped me prepare the cow for our lunch.

After we'd eaten, he got out our bags of gold pieces, and we fell to counting them. There was no need to count, of course, we knew exactly how many there were, but they're so pretty that we enjoyed just looking at them.

We must have dozed for awhile, for the sun was nearing setting when I woke with a start, and prepared to build a fire to roast the boy. But he wasn't in the oven, and then I noticed that a bag of gold was gone as well. I hissed with frustration, which woke Coll.

"Never mind," he said, when I explained the matter. "He bought more than one bean, no doubt, from your rascally cousin. He'll plant another one day, and come back. We'll catch him then."

Several months went by, and I had nearly forgotten the boy, when here he came again. I pretended not to recognize him, but I knew him right enough. Again he was hungry, again I fed him, again I heard my husband's footsteps and hid the boy in the oven.

"Wife!" Coll roared, entering the house in great good humor, "see what I have here."

"A chicken? It will scarcely make a mouthful."

"Don't I smell a strange man?" he asked, sniffing.

"Nonsense," I smiled, nodding toward the oven. "Tell me why you've brought home a chicken."

He returned my smile. "This is not a chicken for eating, my dear. This is a very special bird indeed. Watch."

He put the hen down on the table, and said, "Lay!"

The chicken promptly laid a golden egg, heavy and round and lovely.

"She can only lay one egg each day, but if we feed her well, we'll have all the gold we can ever want," he said. "Oh, and there's a pair of sheep outside for our lunch."

The only way I can explain what happened next is to suppose that two sheep made too large a meal, even for us. Because, though I planned to roast the boy later that day for our supper, we dozed off again. And of course, when we awoke he was gone, and our wonderful chicken with him.

This time we were both angry, and I resolved that next time the boy came I would somehow make sure he stayed in the oven, even if we went to sleep.

One day, a few months later, my husband brought home half-a-dozen goats, and a harp that played lovely music upon command.

"Wife," he said, "I smell a strange man again," but I was at a loss. I hadn't seen the boy, and told Coll so. But he has a keen nose, so we thought perhaps Jack was hiding. We searched thoroughly, but didn't find him.

So I prepared the goats for our lunch, with some leftovers for supper, and then we listened to the sweet music of the harp, which put us to sleep.

"Master! Master!" we heard the harp call, which woke us with a start. There, just running down the path with the harp in his arms, was Jack. I don't know where he had been hiding, but this was once he wasn't getting away. My mouth watered just thinking about having roast boy instead of leftover goat.

Coll seized the ax and ran after the boy, shouting, "I'll get him this time, never fear!" Since this time he could follow the boy to find where the beanstalk came up from below, I was sure he'd have the harp back in no time. He and the boy were soon out of sight, so I turned to building a fire to cook dinner.

I cocked an eyebrow at him when he returned empty-handed, but he was so dejected I didn't say anything.

"That boy," he said, "runs like a deer. I couldn't catch up to him before he had started down the stalk, but I heard him shouting for his mother to bring the ax.

"Aha, thought I, two can play at that game. So while he chopped away at the bottom of the stalk, I chopped at the top, and since I chopped faster, it soon fell away. I hope it dropped on him and smashed him flat."

"And I hope the little villain has no more beans," I replied.

Since we never saw or heard of him again, I suppose I was right.

Rumpelstiltzkin

*H*ad my father not been so eager to bring himself to the attention of the King, and had the King been a less greedy man, I would today be a miller's daughter, probably married to the blacksmith's son.

But Papa, one day as the King drove by, could not refrain from calling out to him, and when the King stopped his carriage to see what was wanted, Papa could think of nothing better to say than that he had a beautiful daughter who could spin straw into gold.

I heard him, and watched the greed spring into the King's eyes, and wished myself in the next kingdom. But it was too late. It not having occurred to the King that if I had such an ability, Papa would be a wealthy man and not a mere miller, His Majesty insisted that I accompany him to the palace to demonstrate my wondrous skill.

That very evening he shut me in a room filled with straw, commanding me to spin it into gold on pain of death. I wept with terror, and anger at my father. How could he have been so foolish? And what on earth was I to do? The door was locked, there was no escape, I faced certain death in the morning, and I but eighteen years old.

Suddenly the door opened, I know not how, and a dwarf entered the room.

"Why are you weeping?" he asked kindly, and smiled when I explained.

"What will you give me to spin the straw into gold?" he asked.

This struck me as a foolish question, since a room full of gold would clearly be of more value than anything I possessed. However, I offered him the necklace that had been my mother's, he accepted, and before morning the straw was a mass of shining gold.

I thought, in my artless way, that the King would be satisfied and would allow me to return home, but not a bit of it. When he saw the gold, the light of greed redoubled in his eyes, and he locked me in an even bigger room, with even more straw, but with the same command.

This time I wept not so copiously, hoping for a reappearance of the dwarf, and was not disappointed. He accepted in payment the ring my grandmother had given me, spun the straw to gold, and went cheerfully on his way. I thought surely the King's enormous greed would be satisfied with a second room full of gold, but not so. He rubbed his hands in glee and locked me in a third room larger than the other two.

When the dwarf came, demanding a reward for his help, I had nothing left to offer. When he asked for my first-born child I realized that was what he had wanted all along. I was young, and frightened, and could see no way out of my terrible dilemma, so I agreed. Besides, I reasoned, who knew what the future might bring?

When the King entered the room the next morning, I decided that as there was no knowing what the dwarf's next demand might be, I had had enough of "spinning straw into gold" for an avaricious monarch. Further, I felt three rooms full of gold ought to have satisfied His Majesty.

I therefore looked him straight in the eye and said, "Your Majesty, I have spun enough gold for you. You are in need, not of gold, but of a wife who will be your Queen and give you an heir."

Imagine my astonishment when the King's eyes glazed as I spoke. I blinked, and he started, as if he had just awakened.

"Beautiful and talented maiden," he said, "will you marry me, and be my Queen, and give me an heir?"

"Of course," I replied, blushing prettily. So we were wed and I became Queen of the kingdom, a position I enjoyed very much. I even allowed my silly father to attend the wedding.

A year later I gave birth to a healthy and winsome baby boy, so all the King's wishes came true.

When my boy was nearly two, I was reminded painfully of my promise to the dwarf, which I confess I had forgotten. Here he came one day, demanding his payment for the third room full of gold. You may believe that I wept then, offering him riches, half the kingdom, anything.

But nothing else would do, he insisted. "I can spin straw into gold, if I want riches," quoth he, "but a living child is what I desire. You are so distraught however, that I will take pity on you. I will give you three days to guess my name. If you do not, I will take the little Prince."

So I guessed all the unusual names I could think of, and of course his name was not Fortunato, nor Melchior, nor Sheepshanks.

He went away chuckling, saying he would return on the morrow. When he left I bethought me of the power I had exerted over the King, and began to look for a solution to my problem. I sought out all the strange names anyone in the palace could recall, with a view to providing the dwarf with some amusement the following day.

None of the names was his, of course, and he left me, laughing aloud and promising to return for the child.

Next day, after I had given him several guesses, all in vain, he became impatient and demanded that I hand over my boy. So I looked into his eyes, watched them glaze, and said, "Tell me your name, little man."

"Rumpelstiltzkin," he replied. An odd name indeed.

"And tell me further," I asked gently, "why you insist on taking my child instead of some other reward?"

"Look at me!" he cried. "I am twisted and misshapen! Ugly! In all my years, no one has ever loved me. If I take a small child, perhaps it can be taught to do so, and if not, perhaps it will make a fine servant. A king's son for a servant! Would that not be a fitting reward for one who spun three rooms full of straw into gold?"

I blinked, and he started. "One more guess!" he exclaimed impatiently. "Only one, I grow tired of this."

"Might your name," I inquired timidly, "be Rumpelstiltzkin?"

At that he stamped his foot and burst into tears.

"Come," I said, "it is not so bad as that." I turned to a screen in the corner of the room. "Come here, Belinda," I called, for I had thought that perhaps the dwarf was merely lonely and not cruel.

From behind the screen came a tiny blonde toddler. "Here is your new father, child," I said.

A smile spread across her face, a smile of such winning joy that I caught my breath.

"Papa!" she cried, wobbling toward the dwarf, beaming at him.

He held out his arms and she staggered into them, clutching him fiercely. He turned to look wonderingly at me.

"She is an orphan," I explained. "A child who is in need of a father's love and guidance. Will you not take her, and leave me my baby?"

Without a word he picked Belinda up, and cradling her in his arms, smiled briefly at me and left. I have not heard from him since that day.